To
a loving friend
of Wayne's
with pleasure
from
Robert Olivier

TINONC

TINONC

Son of the Cajun Teche

by

ROBERT L. OLIVIER

PELICAN PUBLISHING COMPANY

GRETNA 1974

Manufactured in the United States of America
Book design by Oscar Richard

Published by Pelican Publishing Company, Inc.
630 Burmaster Street, Gretna, Louisiana 70053

Contents

Introduction

This book is dedicated to the Cajun himself with the hope that he of our day may recapture from his unhurried past a full measure of the wisdom, the simplicity, and the hidden heroism that he may need to apply towards the rebuilding of America; that he may love his wife and she him, and that together they may share forever the peace that abides in the heart and soul of a God-loving family—their gift to the nation that under God solicits survival at a critical moment of staggering corruption.

It is to be hoped that in the total recovery of his heritage the Cajun will continue to advance in the professions and all learned disciplines and will remain no less American for being sturdily French.

My sincerest appreciation to Mrs. Spencer Gee of Jeanerette, Louisiana, for typing my manuscript and to my cousin Emerite Olivier Perret for proofreading and other kindnesses. I am also indebted to Donald Hebert for providing the lyrics, the translation, and the annotation of the three popular traditional Cajun songs rendered on a festive occasion near the end of the book. Mr. Hebert is music coordinator for the public schools of St. Landry Parish.

Formidable

Everybody in the village of St. Pierre knew that the little boy Tinonc (Bernabe Gaudet) was indeed very strong, that his grip was like a vise which could close and lock and cause others to shed tears of intense pain. In his young hands, as in other parts of his body, there was incredible power such as other little boys did not ever possess.

"*Jamais d'la vie*, Tinonc!" his mama would exclaim in answer to a loud voice of pain. "Make no hurt to you lil brudder, *cher*."

But Tinonc was not a boy like other boys, and his "lil brudder" was no little brother, but a big brother three inches taller, fifty pounds heavier, and several years older. But to everybody, including his mother, Tinonc, with his baby face, was a little old man. Some ladies called him "cute," in all his dignity and innocence and good manners. Indeed he was a ladies' little man and should have been soft, yet he was as hard as rock, and when a half dozen of his peers all together wrestled with him, they could feel as they fell one on top of the other that his body was more like wood than flesh and bone and muscle.

Whence his great strength nobody seemed to know, although certain it was that he received more than a sufficiency of the rigorous exercise best suited to the development of the very hardest muscles. Some of his more distant neighbors were amazed when for the first time they saw him test his strength, his speed, and his endurance against men of physical maturity and experience. Sibec, as a close neighbor, knew much more about this boy than other interested adults, and always smacked his lips and rolled his big eyes and even crossed them when he spoke of Tinonc's feats of strength. *"Formidable!"* he would say. *"Formidable!"* Sibec had learned the word from an old priest born and reared in Normandie, France.

Tinonc's eyes were steel blue and the skin, even on his face, was leathery. The soles of his feet were thickly coated with calluses fully impervious to sticks and thorns and clopped exactly like shoes on a bare floor.

He was never totally clean, but he got wet so often that he could not smell except of the swamp or the bayou and sometimes of fish or bait. His hands must have been clean, all but a few rugged spots that never looked so no matter how violent the scrubbing. He appeared to belong to another world that paid no mind to trivialities of cleanliness, a world that frowned not at all on such as a dry patch of swamp algae on the seat of his pants or an occasional splotch of dry black mud on a shirt that was not white anyway.

His school attendance was in full character, about as irregular as the function of his dollar watch that kept time today but not tomorrow. He called his watch a "biscuit" and had about as much faith in it as he did in his teacher. He told his friends that his teacher talked too much about lessons that he already knew. Also, he hated babytalk in the third grade and had no respect whatever for the mentality of his classmates. For these reasons and several others, he decided to quit school and devote all his time to areas in which his priorities lay.

That decision was not contested either by his mother or by school authorities. In his day parents were mostly illiterate, and compulsory school attendance laws and school buses did not yet exist. Nobody cared too much whether a little boy went to school or not.

Yet, in spite of such limitations, Tinonc was by no means a functional illiterate. It was impossible to determine just how much he did know because he talked so little. It was only on rare occasions that he treated listeners to flashes of adult knowledge.

His father, who could have made a significant difference in his life, had died when Tinonc was almost a baby, and his mother, who was permissive, especially in his regard, made no effort in word or deed to mold his life except concerning religion. Hence in the family he was very effectively assuming the paternal authority; this his mother Armance did not resent or oppose because of results and because of the traditional role of obedience and timidity of most Cajun women. The transition of submission from husband to diminutive son was not difficult for a mother who lived a life of sacrificial giving.

His leadership then was such as to evoke the admiration of all and especially of those who felt sorry for a widowed mother with so many little children and such meager means to sustain them.

What then was there in life for such a mother or

such little children living as they were in an unpainted
tenant cabin far back against the big woods, a goodly
mile from the bayou roadway that wormed its dusty,
rutted course into the village? Was a life of bearing
nine babies in twelve years a life of happy fulfillment
or was it a painful slavery? What were her compensations? Did she laugh when her babies laughed? Was
there pleasure in nursing them, in wiping away their
tears, in soothing their hurts? Was fear tolerable, the
kind that scared you in the night time, that came like
the weird screech of an owl in the very midst of a bad
dream? Was she ever depressed?

Did Tinonc ever wipe the noonday sweat from her
brow in the distant corn patch when the big church
bell bade her rush home to warm the precooked dinner?
Did Tinonc love her or pity her, or both? Did he dry
her face when she so frequently wept for her departed
husband? Did he pray with her when she spoke to God
in the silent movement of her lips?

There was a certain camaraderie of the fields that
existed among Tinonc and his brothers and sisters,
when the babies yet too soft to wield a heavy hoe ran
and played across the rows and turnrows while all the
older ones bent their sweaty backs to the task. The
two youngest would run back home to replenish the
drinking water in the heavy whiskey jugs—to drop the
long well-bucket deep down into the well, pull it up
and release its cool contents into the containers, then
start back toward the group. Did they resent their lot,
picking cotton in the blistering sun? Was it fun to
pack it in the wagon and ride into town for the
ginning, to spend each a whole nickel on two pepper-
mint candy sticks and a piece of black chewing gum,
gomme de mer?

Is life cheating when that's all it has to give? What would the teen-age sophisticates of a later day have to say about such a bill of fare? How would they rate Armance? How would they measure the laughter of the children as they washed their dirty hands and faces before partaking of beans and rice, stewed potatoes, stewed tomatoes, and cold cornbread? Is that the good life to lead so close to the earth—with suntanned faces and arms, with callused hands and fingers and feet?

Madame Sibec, her, she spent a lot of time attending to the business of other people; Madame was always concerned with sex, the sex of other people. Madame said, "Dose girl(s) dey never *courtisent* (date), dey never, *jamais*, go out excep to Mass; dey work, work."

And Tinonc said, "Is it you *affaire*, Madame?" And Madame continued to dislike Tinonc and to talk hereafter in bare whispers about his sisters—because she feared him. She did not even tell Armance about his fight.

"*Pourquoi?*" asked Armance.

"Because he laughed at my sister," answered Tinonc.

"Who?"

"Mimil Arsène."

"Tinonc, wat else?" she questioned.

"I put a handful of dust in his mouth an his face got muddy."

"An wat else?"

"He got a black eye an a nose bleed."

"Shame!" said she, but kissed him on the lips. "We mus wash you shirt so full of blood. You not hurt Emile?" she questioned.

"*Non, maman.* He walked back hoome."

Here she laughed, and he grinned very much like
Jean Ba—and his blue eyes sparkled, and from habit
she bade him go feed the pigs and keep an eye on the
two little brothers who shucked and shelled corn for
the chickens. The pigs stood up against the fence and
squealed, and the chickens squawked and ran right and
left and in circles, and the ducks waddled in the dust
in noisy impatience. Together these birds and beasts of
the bare barnyard continued swirling and giving vocal
vent to their hunger passion until Tinonc threw a
whole ear of corn to each of the voracious pigs, and
the little boys scattered their corn seeds in widening
circles for the quick beaks of the poultry. Then in a
muddy trough the pigs snorted and sucked their
soured kitchen slops as if they might consume the
trough itself.

Tinonc hurried for his syrup buckets from the
kitchen to milk the lowing cows whose calves were
fretting across the pasture fence. He had to hurry
because of Bassette who would surely give all of her
milk to her calf through the fence.

Meanwhile the one horse and the two mules kicked
and bit one another in anticipation of their share of
nutrition.

The best mannered and apparently most sensible
of all the barnyard four- and two-legged animals was
the ancient billygoat who stood aside and did no more
than accidentally topple a skinny old sow that had
blocked his dash for an unseen ear of corn. Tinonc
admired him so much, him with a false dignity and a
sort of humorous wisdom, both so incompatible with
his gross nature and crass depredations. It was nothing
for him to buck from behind any unwary friend or foe

just for the sheer fun of bucking. So like and unlike man are so many of God's lower creatures!

But the home and its environment were not even half of Tinonc's life. His heart and his time were largely given to the great forest and the deeper contiguous swamp, habitats of land and water creatures far swifter and more perceptive in their instincts than any of the barnyard species. He tramped amid the big trees with a shotgun on his shoulder and a dagger at his side; he paddled his noiseless pirogue in the still, dark waters of the swamp.

Such was the boy who later was the close friend of Naquin, Nöel, and Lanclos, who as a man was pitied, respected, feared, and loved by the villagers. What did life do to him in the intervening years? How could he marry such a beautiful wife? How could he father such lovely girls, such sober boys, he who was a compulsive drinker, he who seemed to have no worthy ambition? Was his a wasted life? How did he attract and influence people? Could he be a success and a failure at the same time?

2

Love and Life

Perhaps he could be a success, the kind of success that he prayed for in church, the kind that could come as a person, a sort of incarnate dream.

There was a young girl in St. Pierre who wore a white blouse and a dark blue skirt. She went to the convent school and prayed with rapt devotion on Sundays at Mass. Tinonc always knelt just two pews behind her, and applied a lot of his personal devotion to her and believed that he could merge this act of admiration with his duty to the Lord as a sort of double deed of worship. At least, his conscience did not bother him and there was a feeble hope that some day this goddess could smile upon him and make him very happy indeed.

His most oppressive handicap was that he was fourteen and looked twelve. Would she care? But, who was to pass judgment on his size and the maturity of his affections? Nobody could deny him manhood simply because he was small. He knew the girl and knew her parents and knew within himself that this unilateral love situation did not have to endure.

Of course, there was no question of marriage. He knew that he and she were too young, but could he not live with her distant smiles for three or four years, at least until both were old enough for her parents' consent? Still, he would not be seriously bothered by the world of St. Pierre and the cottonfields. Surely, the woods and the swamp did not care. No advice could he receive from brothers and sisters, because always he, Tinonc, talked and they listened. Not one of them could kill a big alligator and a wildcat and bring them home for weaker people to look at. And so, he kept his own counsel.

Cajuns married young, but who said that he would? The girl had not even smiled yet. Papa Sibec knelt behind him in church and coughed whenever Tinonc was distracted in her direction, not knowing, *enfin*, that he was himself distracted in the process, but she did smile one day and that day was full of glory.

There was a time in his life when all girls, even pretty ones, were rank sissies, *"des p'tites toutoutes en rubans,"* as Madame Sibec used to say. For once Mam Sibec had the right words. And it was no fun to see them play anything but hopscotch at school. They tossed a pebble and hopped around on very stiff legs, but still they were amusing in their athletic rigidity— but only in hopscotch because they laughed at themselves as much as observers laughed at them. Sometimes some of them stuck out their tongues at boys who made faces.

His own sisters were somewhat boyish, yet much too particular about being clean when it did not make any sense.

Still, people married quite young, at fifteen, sixteen, seventeen. So he was told.

Once he had to do girls' housework. His elder
sisters were both sick in bed under the maternal eye
with the mumps. Making beds and scrubbing floors
that did not need scrubbing were the two most disliked of all the household tasks.

Each bed had three mattresses, one of corn
shucks, one of black moss, and one of goose feathers.
All three had to be handled. The top in the summertime was of moss. This was simply turned back to
allow access to the corn shucks called a *paillasse* which
had to be fluffed from four slits and flailed with a
broomstick until smooth. The feathers were likewise
beaten with the broomstick for redistribution and the
elimination of lumps.

The floors had to be massaged with an old broom
with water and *savon d'pays*, then dried with a but-
tonless, discarded, and worn piece of clothing. For a
complete job when the yard was muddy, an applica-
tion of soft, hammered, and powdered brick was considered necessary to finish the drying and receive the
soiling.

Of such was the life of women. Much better off
were they when they were tending the yard or the
vegetable garden, two areas of greater freedom, prov-
inces that should have belonged to men and boys but
were assumed by or assigned to women. This was
productive work and more properly feminine according to Cajun and rural European standards, of which
Tinonc knew nothing.

He was convinced that his girlfriend in church
could do no such work because her little hands were
too white and delicate. He would have to work much
harder or perhaps teach her, God and she willing.
What do you do with such soft hands except powder a

face that needed no powder? What strange creatures were women! It was too bad that his own sisters mattered so little since he could have learned from them.

Still, his major concern was the woods and the swamp and the bayou and the fields—rain, shine, dust, mud, Sundays, weekdays, holidays, Holy Days, coming, going, or just looking. Such was life—and what for? You lived, you grew, you got sick, and poor *chère* mama gave you such unwanted "delicacies" as calomel and castor oil, approved by the old doctor who purged everybody for better or for worse. Green peaches and too many cucumbers always demanded castor oil which meant nausea just from smelling. There were other hideous medicaments unprescribed but approved, all horrible to the taste and disastrous in effect.

The science of medicine was then apparently in its Cajun infancy, and doctors seemed to delight in torture. For a tongue coated a certain thickness or color, the remedies ranged from aloes and rhubarb at one extreme to calomel and castor at the other, with black draught or *régulateur* and epsom salts in between, and if you survived you were lucky that you were cured of biliousness and did not die of pneumonia or typhoid. For malaria, you were given quinine in syrup if you were small and in enormous capsules if you were big. You could live beyond measles, whooping cough, and mumps, if there were no complications. Also, doctors knew a few Latin words abbreviated, and used them occasionally as part of their bedside technique.

The doctor's horse knew all the ruts. He was fat and lazy, and his only diseases were charbon and old age and both were fatal, and when he died, he was given to the buzzards on the bayou bank or in the woods. The doctor's buggy had good wheels and a top of *"toile cirée"* that tilted towards the left where he sat—fat, smug, but not rich. His fees were modest and he dispensed his own drugs, largely patent medicines which could be bought in every *boutique*, and his account books had more credit than cash.

Tinonc's mama had herbs and roots and barks of all kinds, boiled, bottled, unlabeled, usually called *remèdes simples*, and identified generally by their coloring, all in careless competition with the doctor.

One fine Sunday, Tinonc and his mother and all the brothers and sisters, starched and powdered and pretty and barefooted, were walking to church. Armance carried a big rag to wipe all the dusty feet at the public road. Each carried his own shoes and stockings. The boys and girls both wore black stockings rolled and bound above the knee by a *jarretière*. Only Tinonc and Roger, the elder brother, wore socks like men because they alone were old enough to wear long pants. The graduation to long pants was made sometimes by age and sometimes by size according to individual influence upon the parents.

At the highway, all dusted their feet and put on their stockings and socks and shoes. It was amusing to hop around on one leg because of the dew on which no one could sit. Tinonc, his mother, and his sisters had double duty, taking care of themselves and of the younger boys, the youngest of whom had lost a *jarretière*.

"Tiloup ate it," said Tinonc.

"Not true," answered Tiloup. "You, yas, ate it."

"Be sassy an I will spank," threatened Tinonc, with subdued giggling.

The problem was solved with an extra ribbon that Zabette wore in her hair.

All were again walking when Madame Sosthène and the girlfriend drove by, both smiling and both good-looking even without smiling. Tinonc was pleased to believe that the girl's smile was all for him. On such, a man could live.

3

The Living
and the Dead

Seriously a man could not live on love alone. He needed food, clothing, and shelter. He could make and raise his own food and sell moss and frogs and fish and crops for money to buy pants and cloth for shirts and skirts and underwear—to be made by the wife.

All women sewed and all women cooked. But those were things that could be taken for granted. You did not tell a girl you wanted to marry her and hoped she could cook and sew. Well, some day he could visit Madame Sosthène and give her a covey of baby quail, a pretty surprise for her daughter. The best way to court at this time was to win the affection and respect of the mother, and hope that the father approved. This was not too difficult because Madame had told Sibec that Tinonc was strong, brave, and hardworking, and Sibec had told Armance who had told Tinonc. Who didn't know about Tinonc's exploits in the woods and the swamp? And his feats of muscular power were quite spectacular for a boy now going on sixteen.

"Cute!" said Tante Ernestine.

"Wat?" asked Madame Sibec.

"Tinonc," said Ernestine.

"Bête!" answered Madame. "He love Yvonne, pore girl," and with a few vulgar words of total disapproval, Sibec insisted that the girl would do better to marry a *crocodile* or a booll frog, ha! ha! And to think that he gave some baby quail to the mother! True, the little quail were a nuisance and very hard on a hen. They darted through the weeds like insects, worse than ducklings that took to water and left their foster mother on shore fretting and clucking and desperate. Madame Sibec was an expert on matters of maternal frustration. Concerning settings she had full faith in an old hen of good disposition and reputation, one, at least, that ranged close to the *poulailler*. If Mam Sosthène did not have such, there would be trouble. Anyway, little quail eventually flew away and returned to the wild just like pet coons.

"Coons do not fly, Madame," said Tinonc politely but just to be funny.

"Effronté!" said she as she wiggled her left ear and kicked her long skirt, both expressions of utter displeasure.

"How funny!" thought Tinonc as he walked away, not in the least disturbed by Madame Sibec. He had such a feeling of elation and success that a thousand Sibecs could not have disturbed him. This was an evening for the woods and the swamp where man's problems did not intrude, but as night approached he changed his mind and reversed his direction. He would go home and perhaps share his happiness with his mother. He passed her on her knees at her prayers, looking through the window at the distant stars where

God lived. He simply said "Mam" affectionately and went to bed. As expected, the little brothers were sleeping. The two big sisters, of course, slept in a double iron bed in the mother's bedroom, since there were only two bedrooms in the little cabin. There was a little hallway between the bedrooms. Here Tinonc often slept on the floor in the summertime when the heat was oppressive.

This night, the barnyard animals seemed to be restive, awakened by the shrill voices of the guinea chickens, followed by the loud geese and the hogs that grunted and complained in their wakefulness.

Something unaccountably fearful seemed to possess him in his happiness. So compulsive was it that he arose from bed and walked towards his mother's room.

"*Maman!*" said he.

"Wat, *cher*?"

"I worry, *maman.*"

"Go sleep, *cher.*"

And the next day she was dead, stiff in *rigor mortis*, cold and very pale, with unseeing eyes wide open.

"*Maman*, wake up!" he sobbed, knowing full well that there was no waking, that her soul had left her body and had gone to meet its Maker. Could it be that her cold lips would never kiss again or speak again or laugh again? "*Mon Dieu!* She is dead!" That body on the bed was what had been. It was insensitive, forever lifeless. The right hand was hard and as rigid as bone. He tried to lift it up to kiss it and the whole body moved. He put his face against hers convulsively. He asked God why—in French. His breathing became difficult, a deep intestinal function that was almost painful.

He screamed, not knowing that thus he would arouse the whole house. His brothers and sisters came, falling upon the bed and wetting it with their tears, knowing without words that she was dead. He could not stop screaming and did not until his elder sister hugged him, when all at once he realized his awful responsibility as head of the house. He dried his tears and made them all pray—for a whole hour.

Then, one by one, he gave them orders, each a task, and they moved in different directions, obeying without speech, sobbing occasionally as they went about their sorrowful Way of the Cross.

His thinking was still wild and animal-like and controlled only because of exterior necessity. "Mon Dieu!" he repeated over and over again, thinking, "Why did you kill her, God? She wasn't even sick. You took papa first. For wat?"

That tragedy had haunted him for years. As a small boy, he had seen it all, when the mule kicked his father just above the eye, and both eyes popped out full of blood, and blood issued from his mouth and nose and ears, and his body convulsed and jerked as Tinonc fell upon it. Then, of a sudden, it was limp and the breath of life was gone and the soul had fled. The little boy ran in circles around his father, beating off the hogs that could eat human flesh at the smell of human blood. He yelled, too, for his mother, who knew the voice of tragedy and ran screaming and breathless and wide-eyed. Together they carried the dead weight of his body into the house and laid it gently upon the floor and with water and tears she washed his face now swollen and grotesque.

Tinonc took down the shotgun from above the kitchen door, ran towards the barn, approached the

culprit mule and blasted his head off, then suddenly
ran into the woods and as suddenly came back to fall
into the arms of his mother, whom he loved very
much. "I kill him," said he. Not understanding, she
stared at him, and kissed him.

Now she, too, was dead.

And, the people began to come, in pairs and in
families, as they always did, men, women, and children, as they had done for the father.

In the house, some women took charge of the
children; some of them cooked; some washed dishes;
some scrubbed everywhere; and others with experience, acted as undertakers, washing the body and
dressing it in Sunday clothes, closing the eyes and
keeping them closed with coins, folding her hands over
her bosom. Those who had no assignment knelt and
prayed.

The men worked outside, feeding all the animals,
milking the cows. Then they sat on the front porch, dis-
cussing crops and weather, and speaking, too, in awed
tones about death. One man had seen a man die in
church—the man from Jeanerette whose face had
turned blue. Another who used to say *"Tonnerre
M'écrase!"* all the time, was caught on the road in a
bad thunderstorm. He knelt on the floor of his wagon
and swore that he would never again say *"Tonnerre
M'écrase!"* because a flash killed one of his mules and
left an odor of brimstone, of such as hell might smell,
and in fear he went to confession that very day and
told God that he was scared and sorry, but that he did
love Him.

Where was Tinonc? Where but in the woods? "He
kill a mule, hein Tidoon?" asked Jean Baptiste Nöel of

his friend, Tidoon Naquin. Into the woods they went, flushing a covey of quail and three rabbits along the way.

"You answer you question *toi-même*, Jean Ba, an stop counting rabbits on you fingers. *Voilà Tinonc!*"

"Pore Nonc!" said Jean Ba.

"Shut, bouche-toi!" said Tidoon.

And they sat on the log, one on each side with each an arm on Tinonc's shoulder.

"Cry not!" said Jean Ba to Tinonc, who happened not to be crying.

Tidoon rapped his friend in the back of the head with his knuckles to indicate a *faux pas*—with which Jean Ba was very generous at critical times.

Together they brought the young man home and made him go to bed for rest and composure. Tidoon assured him that man is too stupid to know how God works, that bad may be good and good may be bad, that there had to be a heaven for such as Armance. Life is what you make it and death is a beginning and not just an ending.

Then Père LeBlanc came for a second time and he and all the people knelt and said a prayer for the deceased. He embraced and blessed Tinonc and all his brothers and sisters.

4

Those Who Live

After the funeral Tinonc got drunk and went to bed and slept for two days with scant intermission. He had not known until then the full effect of alcohol, but had received what he had sought, a sort of escape from the heavy burden of reality—the shock of a second great unaccountable loss. His friends believed that this drinking, which later became a weekly occurrence, was a strange addiction, since it gave no exterior evidence of intoxication except for a few words mumbled on his walk between the village bar and his home in the field. They knew that Tinonc was "different."

Now fully rested, he would regain control of his thinking and resume his paternal role in the family. His sisters would replace their mother while he remained in the background as disciplinarian.

One day he found Zabette weeping, lying on her bed with her head buried in a pillow. All five of the young boys were in school and Roger had gone to the corn mill with his sister who would stop at the *boutique* for green coffee and a pound of sugar. Most people bought green coffee by the heavy grass sack and sugar and wheat flour by the barrel, but money was now very scarce and Armance had never liked charge accounts which always added ten percent to the annual total.

Zabette was his favorite, blue-eyed, beautiful, and untroubled until now. He had never given her too much of his time or stopped to ask what life might promise her. She had now been to several *"fais-do-do's"* at the *Coin* in his company. Girls went to the dance not with boyfriends, but with members of their own family.

He often teased her about all the boys who had sought to dance with her at the *Coin*. "Stop it!" said he, when she tried to talk in the midst of her tears. "You cry more dan you talk!"

She tried very hard and succeeded for a moment but soon began weeping again and laughing at the same time.

"Stop it!" he repeated. "You cry more dan you talk."

"I do not love Tijean, Nonc. Even if I love, Nonc, I mus not marry. I mus be a mama to the boys. And wen dey are big, I will be an ole maid."

"You will never be ole. You will always be sixteen, *chère*. Laugh not. It is true."

It was then agreed that all would work for the good of the whole family even to the extent of making hard personal sacrifices. Their decision was later applauded by their Naquin, Noël, and Lanclos friends and blessed by the parish priest. As a result, Tinonc decided that he himself would postpone his thought of marriage for several years. To this his sisters did not agree. At any rate, he found it necessary to meditate on his love affair.

Madame Sosthène and Yvonne had come with condolences and offers of assistance. Yvonne nestled a pretty, fluffy, snow-white cat in her arms. The cat reminded Tinonc of his early school days when the teacher assigned him the recitation of a little poem as part of a first grade stage program:

Once there was a little kitty
whiter than snow,
And he used to frolic a
long time ago . . . .

He went home and memorized the verses, but the longer he recited the words, the sillier they became to a *man* who had shot wildcats and chased foxes and raccoons in the big woods.

"Maman," he had said to Armance, "Listen, *chère*, I am a sister, a *toutoute*—'Once there was a little kitty . . .' " and he simulated nausea and ran towards the door.

Seldom was a teacher more disappointed than when he shyly confessed that he could not recite it—with that peculiar finality of his that adults could not contest too easily.

He continued to admire Yvonne in church, but he so often wondered what a big, clean, white cat could do in a cotton patch. In his staunch masculinity, he could find no place for the cat fancier either, and thus he began to entertain serious doubts concerning the desirability of the pretty young girl as a future wife. Could one so delicate survive the pangs of childbirth? Would she even pick cotton? What would Armance have said?

 Pretty girls, Zabette excluded, were so peculiar and so sensitive. They could not fish except from the bank and some were scared of bait, and when they stood up in a pirogue, they squealed in fright because of the *ballottement* which they themselves were causing by their actions. They could not even swim, and when they stepped into mud, their shoes remained stuck. They were a lot of trouble.

He was too busy now with an inner crisis that overshadowed the problem of girls and eventual marriage. This crisis had originated with the death of his father and intensified with that of his mother.

Since both had been buried on Saturday, that day had become evil on the calendar of his mind. Every recurring Saturday evoked the black memories that had tormented him since the first. He felt within himself, in the very bones, a deep depression because God would not reveal why his parents had died. He recalled the man across the bayou whose beautiful and only daughter had lost her life in childbirth. Tinonc could see him still, standing on the bayou bank with arms upraised, cursing God and hurling at heaven all the vilest words that he knew. He could be heard a half mile away, yelling at the top of his voice, using English when the French blasphemies seemed too weak. Neighbors went out of their houses to hear the awful words. He is *fou*, poor devil, they said.

Tinonc was by no means crazy, even under the influence of hard liquor, and it was none of Mimil Arsène's business whether he accepted the landlord's charity or not. Du Clozal was a rich man, he knew; his lands were extensive and the banks must have been full of his money. "You crazy!" said Emile Arsène.

"You go to hell, Mimil!" answered Tinonc. "Wen I have need of you advice, I will ask."

Mimil said, "Aw! Nonc," in appeasement. "I hear

he will feed you family. Nice man!" resumed Mimil,
still blundering.

"A damn lie, Emile, an if you tell one more, I
will give you a goo-od *coup d'pied* to make you shut
up an commence to run."

Arsène said "goo-od bye" and moved fast.

Tinonc was severely criticized for refusing to
accept assistance from du Clozal. Many people thought
that his was a false pride unworthy of one so much in
need. Who was poorer than this tenant family who
lived and ate by the work of their hands, the sweat of
their brows, and the uncertain benevolence of Mother
Earth?

They were poor but there was always an abundance of food in their *dépense*, dried, canned, salted,
and preserved—plain, coarse, but substantial. There
were never fewer than a hundred gallons of cane syrup
per year, many half-gallons and quarts of canned
foods, of tomatoes, okra, eggplant, corn; many half
gallons of preserved peaches, pears, figs, and blackberries. The *basse-cour* yielded chickens, guinea
chickens, ducks, geese, and turkeys. The barnyard gave
pure lard, bacon, fresh pork, salted pork, *boudin*, and
sausage. From the woods, the cows brought milk and
bull calves. True, all were rather shabbily dressed, but
who wasn't?

5

Idyllic

One day while picking blackberries in the woods, Tinonc had come upon a young girl also picking berries. She was alone, wearing a flapping old Acadian sunbonnet and much more clothes over the rest of her body than she needed to pick berries. He could see a face in the deep shadows of the shabby old *gar'soleil.* There were patches in her long dress and bloody scratches on her arms, bare below the elbows. He could not recognize this creature until she called his name. *"Tinonc,"* she called in a voice that had always thrilled him. He was almost shocked to believe that it could be Yvonne—with no companion in sight and at least a mile from her home.

She uncovered her head and face and revealed droplets of sweat coursing down her cheeks, flushed and pink with the heat.

"It is not you!" said Tinonc. "You have no fear? Look at you arms fooll of blood. You mama know dis, yes? You have no fear? You want suicide?"

"No," she laughed, in answer to the last two questions.

"*Mais*, you cannot fight. You not strong."

"I have a gun," she answered, "in my big pocket."

"You can shoot?"

"You wish to see?" She pulled out a big revolver and shot a post on the fence nearby.

"Well, I be . . . ?"

"Walk with me, Nonc, part of the way if you please, and if we see Mam Sibec, run, because it will be a scandal—that old *gazette*. I am so glad, Nonc, to see you here. You have always been my *hero*. Jump the ditch, Nonc, with my berries. Then come back and help me across."

She spoke so well, thought Nonc, and she looked so beautiful. Perhaps it was her school that made her different. Of course, not in looks. She was so much like his favorite sister, Zabette.

He straddled the ditch and took her hand, both unnecessary, he thought, but part of a game which they were both playing. He was so tempted to hold her in his arms and kiss her on the lips, but instead, he simply looked at her and said, "Someday soon . . . " not knowing what he meant. Words did not matter anyway.

"Yes," she answered, meaning, he believed, "I love you, too."

His eyes followed her as far as the trees permitted. Once she turned back and waved at him.

How beautiful was life, how beautiful to discover that she was not at all the picture of feminine frailty that he had painted! This girl could be a partner, walking beside him in the mud and the slush or the dust and the heat, in light and in darkness, in thunder and in rain, in sickness and in health, in life and in death—forever.

That Saturday he did not get drunk. That moment, he knelt near a big tree and said, "Thank you, God."

Would he now need help from du Clozal, not another house but just an added room, perhaps? Surely she loved him. Would she marry him and live in a cabin, mistress of a single room? When?

"If you love her, Nonc, marry her. Monsieur du Clozal will be glad to build a room. She is so beautiful. You are very lucky, my brudder," said Zabette.

And so, there was a purpose in his will and a spring in his step. What would he do next? Go to Madame Sosthène and tell her how much he loved her only child? No! In that sector, he'd let Yvonne talk. Would she?

He would talk to Zabette; she would know just what to do about women. M. Sosthène, him, he didn't matter because he was henpecked. Tinonc did not care too much for M. Sosthène, because he did not like weak creatures; but perhaps M. Sosthène was not weak at all, just a great lover of Madame, who had lost all her babies but one. *Merci Bon Dieu!* for that one!

"Zabette, *chérie*, you know I love you. I have need of help."

"Yes, I know," she answered, "I can see in you eyes. You have talked to Yvonne."

"How do you know?"

"I can see Yvonne in you eyes."

"You rascal! You are so smart."

"Did you kiss her, my lil brudder?" She called him little just to tease him. "Where do you see her? Not in the wood?"

"Yes, all alone, picking berries. No sign of her mama an no sound of Sibecs, him or her."

"My lil brudder, Zabette, me, I will help you, because I love you. I am going to talk to Yvonne an her mama."

"Why cry, my sister?"

"Pore mama!" she replied. "If only living to see you happy! You are not going to leave us, are you, *cher*?"

"No! my sister."

"I will talk to de landlord today an also to Madame Sosthène. It will be a big *mariage* an a big *bal de noces*. *Chère maman* will not mind—so soon. You kissed her? No? I am content," she continued, "because Yvonne is going to know that you have real love. 'Respect,' pore mama used to say, 'respect is love.' Greed is *not* love. She will know, but it may worry her. So, nex time, *cher*, you kiss Yvonne on de mouth for me, hard, on de lips. *Comme ça* she will worry no more."

Tinonc at his age and in his ignorance did not know that restraint is love itself, but he did know that even the lower animals were capable of incredible sacrifice to protect or save their young. Cows were often known to give up their lives for their babies. Of a like quality in man was his devotion to another, a devotion which in its urgency and purity, has in it a touch of Divinity.

6

A La Maison

The home of Monsieur, Madame, and Yvonne Blanchard was typically Cajun, resting upon and where the bayou bank curved to meet the forest. In this curve was a gully, one of many that served the great swamp with much of the surplus water that the heavy rains poured upon the landscape. Always the high land was near the bayou, receiving on its banks the heavier overflow deposits of silt. As the water coursed into the woods and the swamp it became almost free of soil impurities! Invariably the soil near the bayou began as pure silt and continued with a decreasing amount of the fertile deposit until it reached the pure black clay of the woods and the swamp. The process could be done in reverse across the swamp by a similar stream. This seemed to be the geological pattern for many, perhaps all, parts of Acadiana. The Blanchard homestead, then, occupied a very favorable location, considerably higher than any of the neighboring lands, both because of the bayou and the gully.

In front of the house was the standard Cajun garden called a *parterre* which, before the lawnmower, had to be weeded and trimmed with a hoe or a scythe. Poor people seldom owned a scythe. For this reason, the soil was kept bare, and as many flowering shrubs as possible were planted, for the double purpose of beautifying the enclosure and shading the ground to exclude the growth of grass.

From the small front gate leading to the house was a brick walk. The house itself had a porch wall of clay held together by a mixture of black moss and straw. This required very little renovation or repair since it was almost perfectly sheltered. Bluing or *gros rouge* (Venetian red) were commonly used in lime as coloring. The rest of the house was of unpainted cypress exterior. Every interior room was done in the manner of the porch wall with a thin veneer of lime, colored or uncolored.

The *garçonnière,* the attic, was reached by a front porch staircase. In it the boys slept amid a great assortment of materials in storage.

People of means had window panes; others used wooden shutters. Since there were no screens in the early days, all beds were either half-testers or four-posters, so constructed as to hold mosquito bars. When mosquitoes were too bad, the inside and outside of the house were smoked.

The Blanchard house was a classic example of the small, decent, Cajun habitation which for economic reasons contained no more than three bedrooms regardless of family numbers. The more affluent bedded the boys downstairs all together in one room and did likewise for the girls. The parents and the baby occupied the same room, usually small or smaller than the other rooms.

The Blanchard farm contained only fifty acres, thirty in open crop land and the rest in woods and swamp and sloping bayou pasture. Acadians who owned such small acreages were almost as poor as the tenant farmers, but since the Blanchards had but one child they appeared in much better financial circumstances than their prolific neighbors. One man and one woman could not harvest all thirty acres without help—always forthcoming from the large families through a *"coup d'main,"* called "giving a hand" in *Américain*. On such occasions, the hostess and one lady helper stayed home to prepare a great abundance of food, usually a gumbo, with great pots of rice. After the meal, the young girls in a sort of festive, picnic mood, washed all the dishes and took care of all the little ones who needed cleaning.

The Blanchards welcomed the services of a *coup d'main*, because they unaided had only once harvested all their crops in the time that was often so limited by the weather.

When Zabette came by way of the public road, Yvonne was in school and Madame was cooking the dinner which was going to be eaten as supper since Sosthène, too, was away, at the blacksmith shop for the making of a wagon wheel and the sharpening of all his plough points. It took so long, explained Madame, especially to fit the red-hot steel rim over the wooden rim of the wheel. The *forgeron* had to build a circular fire to heat the rim and then to apply it quickly, sizzling and scorching to the wood.

Zabette was not interested and very impatient, and, without preliminaries, told her that Tinonc was *en amour* with Yvonne and would like to marry with her.

"Merci Bon Dieu!" said Madame greatly pleased. "He is so pretty, him, an so strong. Dey could live wit us, hein?"

"No!" answered Zabette. "He cannot leave us wit all de little ones, Madame."

"Yvonne mus not leave me; she is all dat I have. I would die." And she wept.

"I am so sorry, Madame, an I know not wat to say," said Zabette upon leaving.

On her return home, Zabette decided that Tinonc might know just what to do and say. After all, besides Tinonc, there were two other persons concerned: Monsieur Sosthène and Yvonne herself.

Madame Sosthène was a skinny, sickly, nervous, middle-aged woman, who could not live through a single day without *la migraine* or assorted ailments which she called *misères*. Her choice expression was *miséricorde!*, which she did not fully understand but which suited her purpose of eliciting sympathy, especially her husband's. Never was word more abused and misused and overworked. Yvonne apparently had developed immunity to her incessant lamentations, and Monsieur Sosthène, him, was hard of hearing and almost totally deaf in the left ear which he often turned in her direction in self-defense. Poor woman! Her life was a litany of losses, as Sibec, man and woman, used to say.

"When she commence her *litanie*, I say goo-od-bye, me, an go hoome," said Madame Sibec, whose manners were not always perfect.

7

Hope

For Tinonc a visit to the Blanchard home was no task at all. He did not consider Madame a very serious obstacle; he did not fear M. Sosthène, Yvonne was a pure joy, and of himself he was quite sure.

Monsieur greeted him at the garden gate and addressed him as *"jeune homme,"* which had no special significance beyond "young man." M. Sosthène seemed to be in full control of the conversational situation. When Madame sniffled a bit too much, she moved under his frown to another room where she regained control of her emotions. There was no henpecking in evidence. Monsieur, after all, was strong and well-conditioned physically, and Yvonne even accompanied Tinonc to the front gate with no chaperoning except from the father standing in the dim light of the front doorway.

Tinonc held her hand and said "Chérie, I love you," as he kissed her on the forehead.

She answered, "I love you, too. Everything will be all right. Meet us at the road Sunday. I'll make mama walk."

He walked away with reluctance. His joy was

immensely more than imagination had ever been able to create. It was a new experience, the first in a lifetime. It seemed to penetrate and dominate every part of his being. It was like a spirituality, a vibrant holiness that made him pray and glorify the object of his affection.

Yvonne had pale blue eyes that danced in a sort of inner light. She had a soft smile that flickered in her eyes and trembled on her lips, a ready laugh that made others laugh. To him she was lovely beyond words and the picture of her loveliness possessed him in all of his wakeful moments.

On their trysting Sunday they walked hand in hand towards the church. Madame Sosthène's only objection was a frown; Monsieur Sosthène frowned too, because she did. He was displeased, not with his daughter but with his wife. Tinonc and Yvonne in a possessive happiness new to both of them were quite oblivious of time and place. They were even unconscious of the giggling of the little boys.

At the church, their walking party came upon two men, close friends, standing and chatting in the company of a young boy holding in his arms a smaller boy of two named Tidoon, after his father, the younger of the men. These were Tinonc's friends—Jean Baptiste Noël, several years older than his companion Tidoon, and Pierre Lanclos, several years younger than Tinonc. The baby Tidoon was Papa Tidoon's firstborn son.

Tinonc shook hands with his friends but did not tarry, anxious to kneel, not in his accustomed pew, but right next to Yvonne, thus telling the assembled world that Yvonne was the girl that he would marry. Love and sex for him, as for farm people generally, had no deep mysteries, no secrets except insofar as it surpassed animal existence, except in the infinity of joy that it produced.

If such was life, then he could so easily weigh the burdens and measure the gentle peace of his mother's world, her encompassing spirituality that reached everyone around here, her godlike love, not just of chosen neighbors but of all humanity. Strange that this should be to one so ignorant. Yet, beyond a doubt she lived and died in the fruition of God's purpose in creation. Her life was the great "why" of the universe, the elemental beauty of all existence, the reflection of the magnificence of God Himself.

Tinonc had always been so busy and so pleased in his loneliness that he had found no time except in light observation to probe the mysteries of life, but he had always realized even as a very young boy that God moved among His creatures especially because of inequalities that could not be justified on earth.

Those in the animal world did not bother him at all, because there were therein so many compensations. A cat could claw up a tree but a dog could not follow. Without wings most birds would surely die on the earth. The rabbit, with remarkable agility and speed, could save himself.

Among man only immortality gave promise of equating the differences. Why was Sibec so ugly or Tinonc himself so small? Why was Roger so slow in both mind and body? God made men partially ignorant of his personal condition of inferiority, giving him eyes that saw his neighbor but not himself, ears that heard only what he willed.

And now, without Yvonne, he could not breathe. And so he knelt near her and brushed his shoulder

against hers, and, instead of praying, wondered what
Tidoon Naquin might be thinking while probably pre-
tending to be saying his prayers. What would Jean Ba
have on his mind? And Pierre Lanclos, *protégé* of
Tidoon, Jean Ba, and du Clozal, Pierre with a token of
sadness even in his smile?

It was really not hard to know what Jean Ba
would say, or rather, what questions Jean Ba would
ask.

"Tinonc, him, he got a girl, hein Tidoon? Is
purty her, hein Tidoon?"

Jean Ba nudged Pierre and tickled him under the
chin and said "Keeree, keeree!" to make the baby
Tidoon smile—unconscious of tickling the wrong
person.

"It is not Pierre de baby, Jean Ba," said Papa
Tidoon. "You mus not *chatouiller* de wrong man."

"For please, Tidoon," answered Jean Ba embarrassed and irrelevant, "make not a farce on my beard."
Such were the words of the pair when Tinonc, with
Yvonne and her parents, overtook them in front of
the church.

"Sosthène," asked Jean Ba, never one to beat
around the bush, "Sosthène, *vieux nègre*, permit me to
kiss you beautifool daughter in honor of my frien
Tinonc, hein Sosthène, *vieux chien*?"

"Me," said Tidoon intervening, "I answer 'No!'
for Sosthène. It would be *criminel* to rub that beard
and *moustache* on a purty face."

Jean Ba nevertheless kissed her on the chin while
everybody laughed.

"Hap! hap!" said Jean Ba pleased.

8

For Better

Since the episode in front of the church, it seemed almost unnecessary to ask or to tell Monsieur Sosthène that he Tinonc and Yvonne wanted his permission to marry. Indeed it *was* unnecessary because the asking was never achieved. The plans were made as a matter of course. Such so often was the spontaneity of Acadian life, the simplicity and ease of momentous decisions.

Now that an informal engagement to marry was a *fait accompli*, the villagers could talk. Those who relished fiction could add, subtract, multiply, divide, and have a general good time with the arithmetic of the case, present, past, and future. There are always people in every village who play the news for all it is worth, for better or for worse, and there are likewise those who work assiduously to keep the record straight. Madame Sibec was a leader at one extreme and Tidoon Naquin was one at the other. They seldom met in open conflict because Madame's powers of invention were too weak to resist the bold, brutal, and truthful assaults of her antagonist. In fact, Naquin was matchless.

"Tell me, Titante," offered Sibec one day to Tante Ernestine, "how can dat lil *garçon* support a wife, him, wit already a house fool of children left by his *défunte* mama, him a tenant farmer."

"De goo-od God," answered Tante Ernestine, who was very gentle, "is still on de bayou, *chère*. Tinonc an Yvonne an Sosthène are much strong. Work do not kill, hein?" said she in her interrogative statement very common in the speech of all bona fide Cajuns.

"But worry kill," answered Naquin standing tight-lipped and unseen behind Madame Sibec, "above all," he added, "wen it is not you business."

Madame looked for help at her husband who was crossing his eyes without offering any reinforcement. Naquin was much more than he and she could battle. "*Allons*, les go," said Sibec in retreat and defeat.

Under his breath and not to be ugly, Naquin called her an old *guêpe*.

And so, the great day approached with the endless activities of the mother and daughter and sisters. Even Roger had to run endless errands. Tinonc himself appeared unruffled, so adept was he at concealing his emotions. Sosthène confessed that his wife was becoming more of a nuisance than ever. Her migraine had disappeared, but she made so many trivial and domestic demands upon her husband that he had to keep his hands washed at all times. Zabette was so excited all day that she had to remind herself that the coming wedding was not hers but Tinonc's, and the little boys were in a constant state of idiocy, giggling, laughing, pushing, pulling, telling jokes that were not funny and occasionally going so far as to compel Tinonc's disciplinary intervention.

"Shut!" Tinonc would say with a touch of violence in his voice. "Go to bed, now. Sleep, my lil brudders." They knew his tone and dared not disobey. "Wash you feet, *chers.*"

"Say you prayer," added Zabette and Marguerite simultaneously.

In the days when the Acadians were stepping into the accelerating machine age, well past the turn of the century, when the noisy, ugly little Ford cars and pickups were wreaking such havoc in the dust or mud of the three-rutted dirt roads, in those days every man traveling placidly on the highway, when accosted by steel-rimmed wheels, must be prepared to see his horse run away with his buggy or his mules balking in their wagon traces against the roadside fence. It was not uncommon for these mechanical monsters to rattle past a citizen in distress at the incredible speed of thirty-five miles per hour—leaving great clouds of dust in their wakes. Loud demands were heard on all sides for laws to protect the ordinary citizenry against the encroachments of progress so-called. Who would pay for Sibec's fifteen fences ripped by Sosthène's bull in a running hysteria of fear? What man has a right to stampede every living creature along the road with unmuffled rattletraps that could scare anybody?

It is interesting to observe that when a distant neighbor and wife offered their "tin lizzie" to take Yvonne to the church on her wedding day Tinonc said "No." He preferred to begin his wedded life in peace, and so did Yvonne.

Sibec it was who took Yvonne, with Madame sitting as stiff as a statue in between, yet wetting all the bosom of her dress with tears unrestrained. Tidoon

vouched that Sibec's eyes were crossed all the way
from his house to the church.

With Jean Ba came Tinonc, stiff and uncomfor-
table, washed and powdered, in his first new suit,
given by his *parrain*, du Clozal.

Madame du Clozal had not only given Yvonne's
dress but made it herself, and for the first fitting had
called Tinonc to come and behold this stunning creature in immaculate white. Not shy, but hesitant and
almost unbelieving, as in a dream, Tinonc stepped up
and took her in his arms. Her lips were warm and
salted with the tears that coursed down her face.

Madame du Clozal had always loved both Tinonc
and Yvonne. She admired him in his ruggedness and
sterling courage; she admired her in her beauty, her
patience, and her staunch resistance and refusal to be
warped by her sick mother.

"Loo-ok-a-dat Tinonc, *chère pitié*, Tidoon, how
purty, hein Tidoon?" exclaimed Jean Ba.

"Nice it is," answered Tidoon, not conscious of
Tinonc's beauty but more in a mood to philosophize
on the contrarieties of womankind. "Wen a woman is
happy, she cry. Wen a woman is sad, she cry again.
She never make up her mind."

"By damn, Tidoon, we kiss her wen she cry and
we kiss her *encore* wen she laugh," answered Jean Ba.

"Me, wen my *vieille* get me mad, I tink of my
défunte maman, and I get glad *tout d' suite*."

"How in de hell can Tinonc raise two family on a
tenant farm?" offered Sibec.

"Go jump in de bayou, Alphonse Sibec. You
gonna help him, hein?" asked Tidoon, getting angry
and sarcastic.

9

Together

A wedding in Acadiana a generation or so ago was unlike a wedding in any other part of America. It was wide open to the public, and everybody, even babies in arms and feeble old folks, attended. Those who were not *cousins* or *cousines* had to be foreigners or transients or unclassified relatives *par alliance*, and the village, as the church overflowed, became a veritable ghost town. Even the cows, ranging across the deserted streets, seemed to veer in the direction of the church.

But cows or no cows, the radiance of the bride, the unexpected cordiality of both Sibecs, the exuberance of the Naquins, the quiet solemnity of the liturgy, everything and everybody contributed to the memorable beauty of the occasion.

"How do de priest know so much about marriage?" asked Arsène, with his accustomed acidity. "He ain' got no wife."

"Our *docteur* can tell you about four tousand baby an he not a woman, him," answered Naquin, ready for battle.

At this time in history, the Acadians did not

know the meaning of the word "honeymoon" either in French or in English. Even so, in their poverty and pragmatism, it would not have made sense for newly-weds to take off on a spending spree for places unknown and for the dubious purpose of adding a drop to the cup of happiness that was surely overflowing.

To their woodside cabin, then, they went, to spend the day, walking in the woods, and then resting in preparation for the big *bal de noces*, which started promptly at sundown and ended for the married couple at ten or eleven o'clock. The burden of protocol was especially heavy on the bride, who had to be kissed and hugged and danced with by young and old, including the musicians.

It was all very well for relatives and friends to share in your good fortune, to feel through association and communication the superabundance of your joy, but this tribute of love and friendship was, at the moment, like the frosting on the cake of life. The substance in living was in each other, what each would give to the other. As a matter of earthy fact, Yvonne was very tired and Tinonc had experienced more social contacts in one day than in all the other days of his life. If the cabin was not a palace or a grand hotel, at least it was a haven.

When Yvonne awoke the next morning both Tinonc and the sun were up. His fish nets and drag lines and traps were loaded with fish and fur-bearing animals, two sacks full, one on each shoulder. The fish he placed in the wooden cages, weighted down into the water and chained and locked to the base of a big cypress tree. The animals he quickly skinned, bearing only the pelts for light salting, stretching and nailing to the upper wall of the barn.

From the very second morning, Yvonne begged to accompany him through the woods in the mud and in the boat—observing him opening the traps to release the dead animals, pulling up the nets for the frisky fish, laughing together when Tinonc said that fish had no sense whatever, paddling an occasional alligator—a predator who often gobbled a wild duck even as Tinonc shot it. On his first trip with Yvonne, he carried a double weight of fish and animals. What Yvonne liked most of all was to go frogging at night with a carbide headlight, approaching the big amphibians sitting on logs above the swamp water or squatting big-eyed on little hillocks at the foot of the big cypress or the big-bellied tupelo trees. One quick pounce and Tinonc had his fingers fastened on the frog's slippery backbone. Sometimes he would pick a dozen, sometimes more. Once Yvonne tried his procedure, but missed the frog, lost her footing, and fell into the water. That was a tale to tell the neighbors, and one for Jean Ba to call a goo-od farce, hein Tidoon?

The great adventure for Yvonne was an alligator hunt, by preference a big reptile that Tinonc could stab. He always killed a jumbo for the hide and often a small one for food.

Her trips with Tinonc had become a routine until the fourth month of her pregnancy when both agreed that the woods and the swamp were too hazardous.

She then devoted a lot of her time to their room, reinspecting the wedding gifts, especially the quilts, the products of quilting bees when women ganged together to stitch the bright and multi-colored designs of their own making into the heavy, everlasting bed coverings. Yvonne was given eight quilts, enough for a lifetime and a big family, thought Tinonc.

It was upon their last excursion that she got a
view of the "wild man" of the wilderness. Him nobody knew too well, because he was no sooner seen
than lost. He was as bearded and long-haired as any
man could be. He wore rags, patched and repatched
over and over again, one layer of patches upon the
other. He wore neither hat nor shoes even during the
severest winters. In the rain, little rivulets of water
coursed down across his face and wide back. He
looked like an old man but walked, ran, and climbed
trees like a youngster.

He never went to town, and traded only with
itinerant merchants who served the people along country roads and isolated lanes. These merchants drove
their "hacks," general merchandise stores on wheels,
even into the fields. They were carriers of oral news
and written messages to people who lacked the time
or the inclination to go to the villages for shopping.
Their horsedrawn vehicles were a cross between the
covered wagon and the motor van which they later
became. The burden of their business was barter,
mainly chickens and eggs for merchandise.

All kinds of tales concerning the "wild man"
made the village gossip circuit. He could have com-
mitted murder somewhere. Madame Sibec knew that
he had raped and murdered a young woman in another state. He was certainly in hiding from the law.
Her husband, him, he knew that *Charogne*, as he was
called, was very dangerous, because Eusèbe, who had
cousins on the other side of the wilderness, was told
that he had once chased a woman who had turned
against him and shot him in the legs from behind.

Tinonc himself knew more about Charogne than
anybody else. Many times, as a little boy, had he

visisted the mud hut in which the man lived. The chimney thereon was of clay and so was the floor, hard and gray, from a clay that packed like concrete.

Once as a young man, he had paid a special visit to Charogne. He had followed the man's footprints from the spot in the soft mud where his boat had landed, to the fresh landing on the other side of the swamp and by further prints that led directly to the cabin.

"Why did you steal my paddle an two of my fish?" asked Tinonc from the cabin doorway. "Do not lie or I will beat you up. Keep de paddle; eat de fish, but nex time, you will pay. I can make a paddle; I can catch two fish." The man was speechless, his eyes glowing in the semi-darkness of the cabin. Tinonc gave him his back as he walked away, believing that a thief was also a coward who could not shoot from the back for fear of missing.

Upon relating his experience to Yvonne she expressed a wish to see his cabin. Tinonc refused for fear that an armed man could so easily kill him and assault his wife. She concurred.

10

Death

Little did Tinonc realize that his visit might furnish the spur or the motive for the grief that this man might soon bring to him and his family.

People of St. Pierre still talk about the tragedy. So horrible was it that for a whole year women did not pass Tinonc on the street without shedding tears.

It came in the third year of his marriage when already his firstborn son was two and beginning to talk, and his second baby, a little girl, was but two months old, and his wife, Yvonne, was in the fullness of her beauty and maturity both physical and spiritual.

One of her deepest pleasures was to coach Zabette and to lead her into an education that the village grammar school could not render. Through her Zabette had learned to love all the great English classics. She knew Dickens, Thackeray, George Eliot. She had a special love for Scienkiewicz's great trilogy. She had even studied the styles of Oliver Goldsmith and Robert Louis Stevenson. From reading she had progressed to English pronunciation and enunciation, to a close friendship with the educated du Clozals, father, mother, and only child, Marie Anne, who had later married Pierre Lanclos.

Marguerite had not cared for further education. She, like Tinonc, preferred the out-of-doors, the great wilderness. She was physically strong and fearless.

When her body was discovered, it was covered with dirt, and the surest evidence of her terrific struggle was in her black and blue and swollen and broken hands covered with the blood of her assailant. Her body was totally bruised, and death by strangulation was evidenced in the mutilation of her throat.

Roger had been stabbed a dozen times in the back and the chest. His bloody body lay about fifty feet from hers.

Crossing the wilderness, in a straight line, meant a walk through the woods of about a mile on each side of the swamp three miles deep—a total of approximately five miles, two on foot and three by pirogue. Thus had they moved, brother and sister, redoubling their return steps until assaulted not many paces from the water. The pair had completed their visitation of Eusèbe's cousins, Grand Louis and his family. They were attacked probably by one who had witnessed their going.

When at the expected hour the two had not returned, Zabette and Yvonne began to worry. After two hours everybody was nervous.

"I go," said Tinonc. "You, Tiloup, go tell Tidoon, Jean Ba, and Pierre to join me in de swamp. May be dey are lost." This last word he did not believe because his sister had always had a perfect sense of direction and could not possibly have lost her way. For this reason, he did not use his gun barrel as a horn to attract her attention.

He ran all the way to his boat and paddled as fast as he could. A few steps from shore brought him to the bloody body of his brother, sprawled face down upon the earth. He knew then that his sister too must have been dead, and when he found her, he dropped to his knees in a cold sweat and gasping for breath. Her clothing was shredded and partially ripped off her body. He kissed her on the face and hands and moaned more like a wild beast than a human being. Then, he started running towards Charogne's cabin. He knew for certain from the tracks that he was the murderer. He was relieved not to find him in his cabin because he was afraid of the emotional violence that filled him.

Back to his sister's body he went, using the folds of her dress to cover the bare spots. He did not know what to do next. Fortunately Grand Louis's youngest son had come looking for ducks that had failed to return home. Quickly he dispatched the young boy to notify the sheriff's office.

But his friends were the first to arrive upon the scene, all three as shocked and saddened as he was himself. All wept without restraint. Jean Ba was so stricken that for once he had no questions to ask. Pierre was speechless, and Tidoon spoke intermittently without coherence or sense.

With the sheriff and three deputies came the coroner who added rape to Tinonc's findings.

This double killing and triple crime was reckoned one of the greatest tragedies in the history of the civil parish. The sad news traveled by telephone to the parish seat, thence by telephone again to St. Pierre. It was the kind of news, like a unified call to arms, that moved with great rapidity to every corner of the countryside. All the local villages and farms were ready for action. Even outsiders joined the forces of the sheriff's office. A great non-commissioned posse of aroused citizens spontaneously joined the sheriff's men. They fanned out in all directions, a few venturing into the dark swamp, others north and south and on both sides of the marsh, for many miles in the pitch darkness of night—with scant hope of finding the murderer yet driven by a sort of outraged sense of duty to his victims.

Many stopped at sunrise at farm and village houses, begging food for strength to continue their search.

It was not until late the next day that Jean Ba discovered him in an old abandoned sawmill, a mill of the type that followed the supply of timber, moving from one site to another until reaching, as in this instance, a final site that marked the exhaustion of marketable trees in the purchased area. Jean Ba had not even seen the man when a rifle bullet blew off his hat.

He ran, almost crawling, to Tidoon, leaving his hat on the ground and fighting to recover his speech.

"Tidoon," said he to the sheriff. "He shoot my hat"—having recovered his speech before his senses.

"Me, here," answered Tidoon.

Jean Ba pointed in the direction of the mill and walked like a frightened little boy behind the sheriff.

"He will kill you, Sheriff," said he. "Guard you step, Sheriff. He will shoot you. He do not miss."

"He miss you," said Tidoon.

"But not my hat," answered Jean Ba very seriously.

He would have killed the sheriff except for Jean Ba's quick action. He tripped the sheriff and made him move, so that the rifle bullet caught his shoulder instead of his chest.

A shower of buckshot by the deputies ended the encounter. The man was found on the ground, his body quivering in the final pulsations of life.

"Me, I save you life, hein Sheriff," boasted Jean Ba.

"You did," said the sheriff.

"Shame! Jean Ba," said Tidoon. "You talk too much."

"You also," answered Jean Ba. "He kill my hat an also de sheriff on de shoulder, him, hein, Tidoon?"

11

Lapse

Until our day, women who know no better still scare refractory small children with a threat of Charogne, a bad name no matter how applied, a name that evokes the prevalent picture of a black-bearded fiend who murdered in the night by shredding human flesh and spilling human blood.

It was a bad word most truly for Tinonc who wept on Yvonne's shoulder, drunk again, victim of a habit that he had so effectively controlled before. She had no reproaches on that first lapse during their married life, nor ever afterwards. She understood the unbearable compulsion that drove him.

It is not to be believed that the strongest of men are not weak. It was largely because of his wife that he sought surcease in intoxication. He could not bear the feeling of necessary evil; he could not endure the fact of his tortured want, the thinking that he could not avoid, even for her, the violence of emotion clamoring for escape. At times, he would add up the dead—very simply one, two, three, four, very simply and unbelievingly father, mother, brother, sister. God help him!

The liquor was actually less an escape than an aggravation. This he did not understand. It was that his nature seemed to demand the state of distraction produced. Somehow the alcohol enabled him to subdue his emotions and live in a world of oblivion and sleep, until the coming of the reality of light and work of the next tomorrow. He slept at her side and she did never wake him.

It was many years later, with the faithful Yvonne at his side, that he achieved a notable victory, celebrated one day, at his request, by a vast assembly of his people and friends.

Jean Ba in his unlettered simplicity did not ever fail to remind him that some day he would grow up and be a man. Jean Ba was so naïve that it was practically impossible for him to give or receive insult. His juvenile candor produced laughter but never hurt. In his most serious moments, there was still a suggestion of humor just beneath the surface.

Like Jean Ba, but to a much higher degree, Tinonc in spite of deep sorrows lived with a very active sense of the ridiculous. He was by nature happy and peaceful and deemed so fortunate in his marriage to Yvonne. When the pressure of his losses seemed unendurable, she stood by him with words or deeds of consolation, and when nothing looked feasible, she did nothing—giving him the eloquent silence that he needed.

12

The Great Flood

Perhaps it was not for ill that the great flood came. Though adding to the accumulation of disaster that beset Tinonc, this blow, together with Yvonne's gentle touch, reactivated him for the man's work that lay ahead.

He was among the first to place all furniture and clothing in the cabin attic beyond the reach of the greatest possible flood. His mules he hitched to the wagon, full of chicken coops and feed. For days he and the boys worked in the crib to elevate the corn and secure all the implements in the hayloft. Two of the boys drove the wagon through the single gap in the wilderness, a narrow roadway that ran across a crude bridge over a gully in midforest and then coursed on towards the south and the gentle hill that marked the end of the great Mississippi–Atchafalaya basin. On the very top of the bluff was the home of a friend who had invited him to seek shelter there and even divided his animal lots for the elimination of the constant fighting of displaced animals—and for separate feeding.

All of his close friends had likewise gone south instead of north. Tidoon at the time of their exodus was gravely ill, and Susette, Jean Ba's young daughter, had died and saddened all of St. Pierre.

Tinonc began to think that man was assuredly born to die, and he began to count again, adding one to make five.

Yvonne was left in charge of the family on the hilltop while he returned to St. Pierre to offer assistance to those in need and to await the crested impact of the flood waters.

The crest came in the night, taller than a man, covering all of the crops, engulfing houses, barns, fences, stores, animals, people—destroying in a few unspeakable minutes the work of many years—killing, drowning, tearing, without hands or feet, but lusty and evil and inexorable.

In his pirogue, Tinonc was seen all over town. He was wet and dirty and hungry, but at the service of the villagers. In Arnaud's store he caught a man looting. He stripped him of his booty and ducked and nearly drowned him for punishment. "Go!" said he, "and come again wen you are thirsty."

The man had a boat full of stolen goods. This Tinonc capsized before escorting the thief out of town.

He wept for young Susette; he wept for his friend, Jean Ba, and for Madame Jean Ba, and for all the family. And he laughed with Tidoon, because Tidoon was recovering so fast from an accidental gunshot wound—Papa Tidoon, refusing to be evacuated and fishing from an attic window of his house.

For Tinonc it looked like the water would never leave. As it ebbed, the rains came, greater than he had ever seen, like solid sheets from suspended lakes in the sky.

"De goo-od God is mad," said Tidoon. "He punish us, perhap, because we are bad."

"You," answered Jean Ba.

"Us," said Tidoon. "Do you know dat some people in St. Pierre are hungry even now."

"If you help me," offered Tinonc, "we will wire de bayou, an I will feed dem."

13

After the Deluge

Never had Tinonc worked harder than with the fish and never had anyone seen so much fish. His great nets were filled hour after hour for days. People came by the dozens, lines of them, white and black, young and old. The little man who served them accepted no money.

More work awaited him in the fields and at home. All crops had to be replanted as soon as the soil dried. The water wells had to be scrubbed and treated and dried and rescrubbed and tested. The houses had to be completely disinfected, washed, and rewashed. The buckled floors had to be replaced.

It was not reconstruction that concerned him the most, but personal advancement. Would he live forever in grinding poverty? Not that he cared, but that his wife and children deserved more. What could a man do without education? This problem followed him wherever he worked, wherever he went, until one day he came upon an automobile stalled by the roadside. The owner was in desperate need.

"I am not a car mechanic," said Tinonc, "but I can fix a steam engine, a gasoline engine, an I can make a horse run wen he is lazy."

In ten minutes the car was running.

"I know wat we can do, Tiloup. You open a shop by de road an I will show you how to work."

Some of his other brothers were among the first to buy little pickup trucks for sales trips to New Orleans. Pioneers were they in the marketing of sweet potatoes by truck, selling at first only culls to the merchants of the French Market and returning with tropical fruit for the village markets along the highway.

Tinonc encouraged his brothers but himself could not participate in a commercial venture that required too many days away from his growing family. He was pleased, however, to know that his gifts and skills could be held in reserve perhaps for a more generous future.

One job demanded another. No sooner had he completed one than he faced another, and so many of these had nothing to do with making money. They were like a face that was washed today and again tomorrow, again, again, and again for ever and for nothing but to be clean and possibly to look good.

When field work was completed, all hands had to move into the woods to cut wood for the fireplace and the cooking stove, big pieces for one and small pieces for the other. This had to be hauled and stacked against the backyard fence. Besides the firewood he had to keep a surplus of dry cypress logs, placed in readiness in the swamp, for floating when the big rains and the high water came. Some were split as shingles, others as pickets for the garden fences.

The harvest year of the great flood was not as bad as feared. Much of the work and expense had doubled and redoubled, but a normal yield justified all efforts. Tinonc paid his bill at the commissary and was happy to realize that he had suffered no great losses.

But his gnawing urge to succeed, to work his way out of farm tenancy despite a double family of five brothers, one sister, two sons, one daughter, and many more to come—this urge was always upon him, a moving interior presence, relentless and real, but never surfacing. Yvonne, although very perceptive, could sense nothing in him but a light occasional disturbance unworthy of attention. Her love was serene, her life was full, her health was perfect. Her part, as she knew it, was to assist him with the rearing of two families. The brothers were no problem, and Zabette was a delight, now planning with du Clozal assistance to complete an accelerated high school course in order to qualify for nursing school. The young brothers were very pleasing in their docility and in their ambition to rise above their station in life. Three of them were partners in a part-time auto repair shop, and in a fall potato trucking business. The younger two were full time farm workers with Tinonc.

14

Flappers and Hunger

Between the great war and the great Depression, there was a hybrid period of adjustment that knew not how to cope with new economic, moral, and technological problems. It was the ugly era of the big alcohol stills with their multiple barrels of corn mash and corded firewood hidden in the untrodden woods. It was the era of rum running with its elements of adventure, rebellion, and defiance of the federal law enforcement agencies. It was the day of speakeasies in dark urban alleys, of racketeering in the big cities and of hijacking on the rural highways, of gang killings everywhere. Side by side with criminal big business were the small operators—minor distillers and bootleggers who worked from corncribs, homes, and country general merchandise stores. They produced a colorless raw whiskey with a "kick" so strong it was called "white mule."

A few Acadians grew rich from these ventures, and a few went to federal jails, especially after the repeal of the Prohibition amendment and the accompanying congressional enforcement act, when the licensed liquor dealers became federal informers.

Most Cajuns who participated in the illicit traffic

had only a minor sense of guilt, because they considered Prohibition an injustice, a war measure that
was promoting a massive wave of lawlessness.

Along with the general post-war moral relaxation
came the new behavior of too many young women—
loud, rude, and bold in public places.

In retrospect, the sins of the twenties, except for
city crime syndicates, were minor compared to the
excesses and decadence of a later day. The counterpart
and predecessor of the women's liberation movement
did not go far beyond tight dresses, coarse language,
and occasional immodest exposure. Young girls of the
"new morality" of that day were called flappers, possibly a jocular exaggeration of their resemblance to
birds. They did appear flighty and fickle and they did
invite the harsh criticism of their elders at a time
when there was no generation gap. Boys also were
guilty of such minor follies as swallowing unmasticated
live goldfish.

Country towns and villages were scarcely touched
by national trends. In the absence of radio, television,
superhighways, and universal affluence, evils did not
become epidemic then as now. St. Pierre and Tinonc
were unaffected.

The giddy twenties in Acadiana suffered a sudden
and violent death at the hands of the great flood of
1927 and the crash of the stock market in 1929,
followed by the consequent economic collapse.

The local flood was a simple matter of reconstruction, but the Depression was an extended and
complex period of many-faceted experimentation from
which America recovered only with the outbreak of
World War II.

Jean Ba said that Tinonc could eat his own frogs

instead of selling them. This was only partly true; his market continued at a depressed rate; big frogs brought small prices but big dollars. As the frogs, so went the fish, the pelts, the crops. But Tinonc and Yvonne had the real answer to an economic depression: they lived at home on the products of their own labors and bartered for necessary commodities. Much of what could not be sold, could be eaten, including surplus bullfrogs.

An earlier and even greater disaster was the drouth of the mid-decade, so extensive that it produced the popular song "It Ain't Gonna Rain No Mo'," sung by the young people in a calamitous, semi-humorous mood.

The air everywhere was thick with dust, smoke, and bloodthirsty mosquitoes. The dry marshes near New Orleans were burning deep underground. Farm and plantation pastures all over Acadiana were dusty and cracked, and Tidoon averred that his cows were giving dry milk.

Jean Ba said, "De sun try to set at *midi*"—in reference to the obscurity of midday.

"An de chicken are crazy," said Tidoon. "De only men wit crop are Tinonc an Pierre Lanclos," he added.

Du Clozal had released water from his rice fields to supply Tinonc and Pierre, one a protégé and the other a godson. The rice people in many instances flooded adjoining row-crop lands and thus saved some neighbors from failure. This occurred on a minor scale because the rice during the drouth demanded incessant pumping with no water surplus whatever for any other crops.

15

A Challenge

The long street of St. Pierre had been proud of
its gravel surfacing and so happy to be wishfully out
of the mud and dust forever. Jean Ba and Arsène had
argued the point of which kind of surfacing could
produce the most dust. Of course the argument was
unresolved because there was no possible way of mea-
suring the past dirt against the present gravel.

It was Tinonc who drew the conclusion for them:
"You are both wrong because de brain of Emile is
leaking out of his left ear and de beard of Jean Ba is
fool of sand and rocks instead of dust. Besides, dis is
de firs time dat Texas come to Louisiana. Emile will
plug his ear and Baba will mow his beard an Arnaud will
shovel dust an rocks out of his store, an if you both
get lost, Tidoon will send his bloodhound to find
you."

"You are more bad dan Tidoon," said Jean Ba to
Tinonc, "to make a farce on my beard."

"It is a haircut dat I want," said Tinonc to
Mimil, the barber, and sat in the high swivel chair.

The tonsured young man walking down the street
just a few minutes later was something of a curiosity
even in his own village. Nobody else walked or talked

or laughed or got angry like Tinonc. His anger was as quick as lightning, a sudden flash across his face. He sprang like a cat and hit like a mule, then walked away with steps too long for his legs, the gait of a man accustomed to walking behind the plow.

At the bridge that spanned the sluggish bayou, he met Eusèbe of the green eyes, the crooked nose, the long, skinny arms, and the lips beginning to flap and crease over the open spaces of dental extractions.

Eusèbe had a great, extroverted sense of humor and laughed more at himself than at his jokes, which were not funny.

"*Bonjour, vilain,*" said Tinonc. "It seem to me you could be better hoome working dan on de street wasting time an scaring people wit you ugly face."

"An you, Nonc, you go goo-od?" asked Eusèbe, paying divided attention to Tinonc's words. "You ugly *toi-même*, Nonc."

"Go hoome," said Nonc, "an work you crop."

It was a bad year and Eusèbe had lost most of his crop for lack of rain. "No crop," he answered. "No grass, no cotton. Dust! Dust! It is *malheureux* wen we have only dust to eat. Loo-ok, Nonc, de man who come to fight. Fight him, Nonc," urged Eusèbe.

16

Fight

The big man was a barnstorming prize fighter and promoter of boxing matches among the citizens. He had been told about Tinonc and had looked for a suitable antagonist for Tinonc, but no one, big or small, was available. The promoter's only alternative, a matter of policy, was to issue the challenge himself. He was a real heavyweight, a tall, barrel-chested man of bulging muscles and ferocious mien. The few boys accompanying the big man were thrilled over the prospect of an interesting match, but Tinonc was disinterested and finally consented only after a half hour's prodding by his friends who had joined the group.

The match was scheduled for the next day.

The gloves were so light that the contest looked barefisted.

"I would prefer not to fight," warned Tinonc, "because I have fear you will be hurt."

"Son," replied the man, "go home and tell your mama that you got a yeller belly."

"For dat, *mon ami*, I will knock you out," promised Tinonc in anger.

The exhibitionist guffawed. It did look a joke for two such unlikely opponents to meet in a ring.

Tinonc knew nothing about boxing, but it was an article of living faith with him that nobody could knock him out with a fist, and that contrariwise nobody could resist a shower of his own fists no matter where they landed anatomically.

All of the village men and boys were in attendance when the contestants squared off and shook gloved hands in the center of the ring. Not one villager except Arsène doubted the outcome.

The big man looked professional; the little one seemed grossly out of place and tremendously outclassed

"He gonna kill Tinonc," shouted Arsène.

"Tinonc is mad, mad," said Tidoon.

The big man danced around on big feet while Tinonc advanced upon him like a cat stalking a lion.

"Tinonc will hurt him, hein Tidoon?" offered Jean Ba. "Tinonc look angry, him."

The big boxer, after two rounds of dancing and prancing, finally cast anchor in a corner. His delaying tactics served the purpose of giving the people a reasonably long show for their money. In due time and suspense, he would not only knock out the "little boy," but send him flying through the ropes. What a gift he would be to his nagging people!

In a few minutes now he would open up and put an end to this little comedy. He would wipe the smile off the boy's face, the face that was beginning to disturb him, for never in all his ring career had he found it believable that such a small man could wield such large determination on a face almost innocent in its fearlessness.

Well, if he didn't know any better, whose fault was it? Here goes! He sent a wild, horizontal haymaker, like the mighty sword of Goliath, at the luckless little David. It was aimed at Tinonc's head as if to sever it from its body, but the head had ducked below the breeze of the powerful swing.

The villagers laughed in vociferous concert and so angered the great man that he sent a reckless volley of lefts and rights all over the ring, in mad pursuit of his opponent. He churned the atmosphere with the fury of his assault and did all that he could to land just one blow on the elusive Tinonc, who now at last and suddenly stood still and, with one quick blow at close range, chopped the man's long arm above the wrist. Nobody saw the action that broke the arm, or the next that caught the giant below the chin and felled him to the floor like a big swamp tree. The fight was stopped; a man with one arm could no longer fight.

Such was the unequal combat that cancelled the rest of the evening matches and sent the showman packing for hospitalization and a luckier stand somewhere else later.

Tinonc jumped out of the ring, accepted the plaudits of his friends and hastily returned home to apologize to Yvonne for having engaged in a prizefight.

17

Eusèbe

"You had no choice, *cher*. I am so glad Eusèbe did not box. Poor thing! He would have done so just to please you, and he might have gotten hurt; he's had enough bad luck."

Fortunately Eusèbe's friends did not know about the next impending disaster, not yet very far in the future. Luckily they had been able to catch their economic breath before the crash of the stock market and the long years of economic depression.

In the war, the drouth, the great flood, in hunger and in want, Eusèbe himself had no worries. His long face was becoming wrinkled with age and creased with the smiles that ever played thereon, rain or shine.

It was the day after the boxing that Eusèbe met Tinonc at the bridge.

"Loo-ok," said Eusèbe, "loo-ok wat I see, Tidoon an Jean Ba, *quelle paire!* Be damn! Loo-ok, Tinonc—Jean Ba an Tidoon."

"How come you say it twice? One time was enough."

"Aw, shuck! Nonc. Loo-ok, Nonc, de lil boy Tidoon. It is purty, hein Nonc?"

The three stopped and all shook hands. Little

Tidoon was indeed "pretty," the image of his papa, with a face full of innocence and mischief.

"De dry wedder," said Tidoon, "bring everything bad, dust, mosquito, an Eusèbe."

"Ha!" answered Eusèbe, exposing his upper tooth in a broad laugh that moved his Adam's apple up and down.

"All de time," offered Jean Ba, "Tidoon, him, he make a farce on Eusèbe, him. Tidoon make a farce on Eusèbe, him."

"An you too," added Tinonc. "One day Eusèbe will get mad an bite somebody."

"He can bite," said Tidoon, "but he cannot chew."

"Ha! ha!" answered Eusèbe, and "Hap!" answered Jean Ba, fearful that either Tidoon or Tinonc or both might point their banter in his direction.

The two friends with the little boy moved on while Tinonc and Eusèbe walked slowly in the opposite direction, on towards the big Arnaud store, always the mecca of men in search of news, men even from the farms, so often victimized by weather extremes, idled either by ground too hard and dusty or too soft and muddy.

In their category Tinonc very seldom belonged because he was a man of multiple interests whose every day except Sunday was a work day of sunrise to sunset, in the fields, in the woods and swamp, in the yard among the domestic animals, in the house with the wife and children. To them he went for companionship, for recreation, for pleasure.

Never for long did he leave his family. No matter how far he went and for how many hours, he was ever on his return to the family and the magnetism of home.

Ever since his first love for Yvonne, he saw people and places and things with her eyes. Now, walking down the village street, he did not forget her presence in spirit at his side. Marriage, he believed, was a sacred thing and ever so lovely.

"My wife, I love you!"

"Hein?" asked Eusèbe.

"I was talking to Yvonne."

"You too?" asked Eusèbe. "Me, I talk to my wife in my sleep, ha!"

How Emile would laugh and blabber if he knew how much he cared for his wife! "Stop talking, Eusèbe. I cannot think wit you."

"Aw! Shuck, Nonc!"

Sometimes he wondered if other people were like him, had the same worries, the same drives, the same fears. Was Eusèbe in fact as he was in appearance—this man without guile who seemed to live in a happy, untroubled, juvenile innocence? Without reason, he felt sorry for Eusèbe.

"Goo-odbye, Nonc," said he. "I go hoome, Nonc."

Both walked toward the store, full of people. Tinonc stopped but Eusèbe continued, his skinny back and bony shoulders moving up and down to the rhythm of his long steps.

Tinonc had a feeling of wanting to detain his friend, a sort of premonition of evil! "Be careful!" he called, out of hearing.

18

The Store

What did Yvonne think of the people, socializing as they were in the big village general merchandise store? Friends, cousins, acquaintances were they all. So many were cousins that cousins did not seem to matter unless they were first or second.

Today there were more men than women. Men were oftener in town than women, who could seldom leave home because of the children—those women who were older and had adult children often lacked the inclination.

When men crowded the store, Madame Sibec could not stay too long because she was allergic to tobacco smoke, especially from Aristide's pipe, which she called a smokestack.

On this occasion, Aristide was puffing so vigorously that Madame turned on her heel and went back home in a huff, and left her purchases to her husband who mumbled in protest and crossed his eyes for two days thereafter, according to Jean Ba.

Tinonc knew that Yvonne would be amused when he told her about the Sibecs and about Grand Rouge who was as ugly as Eusèbe and whose hands were rough and covered with long hair and reddish

brown freckles and splotches. Yvonne did not know
Grand Rouge, who had only recently adopted the
village *par alliance.* Tinonc bowed to those women
who were not *cousines.* Mesdames' faces all were white
because of their Acadian sunbonnets which protected
them against suntanning which was not fashionable,
not *à la mode.*

Tante Ernestine's bonnet was distinctive, so long
that it might have covered all of a horse's face, not
that her looks suggested a horse, because her face was
smooth and regular and her eyes were a soft, gentle
blue.

"I would kiss you, Titante, but I have fear to get
lost in de dark of you bonnet."

"How is you beautifool Yvonne, *cher?*" she
asked, ignoring his words.

"Perfect," he answered.

"Nex time, bring her wit you so we can admire
her beauty."

"I am too jealous," he smiled as he walked
towards the door.

There was Emile Arsène coming in and just behind him Tidoon and Jean Ba, the two inseparable as
always. He and Yvonne loved Tidoon and Jean Ba as
much as they despised Arsène.

Tinonc remembered this occasion so well because
Mimil, not having seen him, had wondered in a loud
voice how he, Tinonc, could support a wife and so
many children as a farm tenant. It was characteristic
of Arsène to criticize and even degrade those neighbors
of whom he was envious. He liked a big audience and
he pitched his voice to match the number of his
listeners. He had not seen Tidoon and Jean Ba who
were talking to Tinonc not five steps behind him.

Tinonc was thinking that Yvonne would not like a scene, knowing so well that Arsène's ailment was terminal and would not respond to any social medication whatever. He whispered to his two friends and all three advanced upon Arsène and stood before him stiff and silent. "Say that again. Talk!" said Tinonc, his face clouded and flushed with anger.

"Talk!" echoed Jean Ba.

Mimil walked instead. He turned on his heel and walked out of the store.

An awkward silence had fallen upon everybody including the Sibecs. Madame Sibec had just returned to coax her husband back home.

Arsène's question seemed to be directed at her and she was stammering her response when Tinonc appeared. His presence and his command so confused her that she froze in her position, opening and closing her mouth without words. Her embarrassment was compounded by great new clouds of tobacco smoke issuing from Aristide's smokestack. Finally Sibec managed to guide her out into the street.

"Better to stay hoome," said he.

After making a few purchases, Tinonc walked slowly towards home, with the pain that words of injustice never failed to bring and with the feeling of depression evoked by the memory of his misfortunes and always stimulated by reverses of any kind. It had become a habit to apply two remedies to his condition: one, the secret of future success that he shared with du Clozal and Pierre Lanclos, the other, the great love that he bore for Yvonne. Someday he and Yvonne would stand tall before the villagers and say, "This is what we have done." She would still be beautiful in middle age. Her beauty was everlasting because it was of much more than just the body. What would he be today without her as wife and gentle counselor? A hopeless drunk, perhaps, a man without ambition with nobody to work for. Would he have abandoned his brothers and sister? Would Zabette be in nursing school now engaged to marry a young doctor? Would he have helped his young brothers in their business and pointed to them the way to success? He was still fighting his habit and his conscience. Yvonne still prodded him in silence towards success.

19

When Eusèbe Falls Tinonc Scores

These were Tinonc's thoughts as he walked slowly down the road until he had left the village and come to a clump of live oaks that marked the beginning of the du Clozal estate. He was looking towards the plantation house in a setting of more and even larger live oaks, several hundred yards from the highway at the end of a tree-bordered lane.

In his line of lower vision was the highway itself and the usual shallow ditch. In the ditch was the body of a man, face down and still.

"*Cher Bon Dieu!*" Was that Eusèbe? "Not dead?" He had always felt so kindly and protective towards Eusèbe, as one might feel towards a little boy who needed a friend. With a feeling of numbness and fear, he knelt to examine the face and take the pulse. The body was limp and living. Blood smeared most of the face and still issued from a deep wound in the forehead.

Certainly this was not foul play on the public road in broad daylight. He remembered not to move the body. There was nothing he could do but stop the flow of blood with shreds of Eusèbe's shirt and await the arrival of Augustin, known as Googoose, coming on horseback from the direction of the village.

"Go get de doctor, Googoose," he ordered.

"Wat he got?" asked Googoose.

"Blood," answered Tinonc.

Before the doctor's arrival, Eusèbe opened his eyes.

The old doctor was a man of many words, especially long professional ones that would impress the layman with his great knowledge and competence. He washed Eusèbe's face and wound with alcohol and made him swallow a sedative without water and said, "Now you will *dodo, cher*, sleep, and Tinonc will hold you in his lap, and we will take you home to bed and tell your wife you are damn lucky that a twenty-two bullet just grazed your *nom-du-père* and hurt Tinonc more than you, and if you make a good crop in the fall, bring me two hens for a gumbo if you have no cash after paying your debts, *cher*. Tinonc, that last baby of yours was a whopper. As soon as he hit the air, he yelled like a tiger—with eyes closed tight. I didn't have to slap him. That little wife is a beauty. *Au revoir*, Madame, and you, Easy, take it easy and when you are up, go find that kid who's been shooting and missing song birds and hitting people. You can be sure he'll lie to you."

"*Au revoir*, Doc," said Madame, embarrassed by Eusèbe's loud snore.

Once again on a Saturday, the shock of finding the stricken Eusèbe was more than Tinonc could bear. The episode was so clearly reminiscent of other evil days that it pulled him inevitably towards the saloon. "Yvonne, I'm so sorry. I am so weak."

He believed very firmly that he was weak, as people do who are harrassed and depressed by a long series of misfortunes. Yet, who was stronger in other areas than this little man of steel?

The saloon was a very ordinary frame building which he knew so well from the days when as a little boy he had sold empty wine and whiskey bottles to the bartender at the back door. It was not too clean inside or out, but it did not smell of dirt or dust but of something sweet and pleasing that in a strange way appeared to belong to the sawdust on the floor and to the slick counter that the barkeep continually and unnecessarily wiped with a damp cloth.

When he opened the door, Bouqueta, the bartender, was wiping the counter. "Come in, Tinonc," he said in French. "Rentre ... A *bouteille* of whiskey, *cher*?" he asked uncertainly.

"*Non*," answered Tinonc. "Wat I want you cannot sell. I do not desire to talk, Bouque; I want to run." As he walked out and closed the door, Bouqueta said, "Be damn!" inquisitively.

Walking out into the fresh air of freedom, Tinonc felt the strong, spiritual, almost physical presence of his wife. It was as if her breath was against his ear, sweet and warm and pure as always. So strong was her presence that it prompted him almost to run towards home. She was waiting at the door, having seen him in the distance. She was radiant and conscious of his victory and her soul was full of great joy.

20

His Helpmate

The wonder of it all was how a man so strong and sensible could be enslaved by a habit that belonged to the weak. There was a man in the village who went on an alcoholic binge once a month, flat on his back for days until complete loss of consciousness and transfer to an institution. Tinonc's habit was controlled in time and place, yet was compulsive.

In the hours that he spent alone, especially in the swamp, he meditated in great depth upon all his problems and always found his greatest comfort in his wife. He had never dreamed that he could marry a girl of a higher culture than his own, not that social classes were too well defined in the village, but people with social standing and even people with money only were exalted for the simple reason that man anywhere is ever in search of someone or something higher, some hero or ideal, even false.

In Yvonne he had found the realization of all his dreams, and he loved her with a greater love than he had deemed possible. He used her as a shield in his thinking against the bitterness and tragedies of his past. He often went to her as a little boy might have gone in distress to his mother.

Most marriages fall into the rut of the common-place. Routine becomes a way of life and routine so often grows into indifference. Without the scholarship of psychology, Tinonc knew that his relationship with his wife could never be dull, at least on his part. She on her part matched her knowledge and feelings to his level while slowly achieving a higher equation.

The ugliness that encompassed too many people in America was never their lot.

The regularity of her pregnancies did not depress her because all of her babies were passionately wanted extensions of her beloved husband. Large families in rural America were the rule and not the exception and most women accepted their child-bearing lot as bless-ings and not burdens.

Yvonne was aware that many women would pity her and possibly ridicule her, but she was fully satis-fied that she did not need words to tell the Cajun world that she was happy.

She and he both shared the belief that children could grow and prosper on hard work and love of God and man.

21

Life Hard and Simple

Between the flood and the financial panic of 1929, Tinonc and Yvonne had managed to put away considerable savings, and at the first sign of crisis had removed their money from the bank to du Clozal's big safe.

Very innocently they and all the people of St. Pierre had drifted into the beginning and the continuance of the bad days of the early thirties. They had both learned the lesson that du Clozal had taught, that those who did not owe did not have to fear since they would not have to pay inflated debts with deflated dollars. Hence a depression was not to be feared since it had been their way of life by preference. Certainly they knew nothing about financing, high or low, and when those in the big cities who worshipped the dollar began in panic to drop out of the high windows to the paved earth below—Tinonc and Yvonne did not quite understand.

Their little boys as they grew big enough shucked and shelled corn and carried the big sacks of grain to the mill for the meal that meant bread and the chops that meant feed for the poultry and the pigs which were their source of meat.

Cornbread, sugarcane syrup, fat hens, skinny-legged fryers, milk from the cows that fed on grass and hay—these were their practical nutritional necessities. Dresses came from the bolts of variegated cloth sold by the village merchants. Most of the underwear worn by the little boys and girls was stitched by Madame Sosthène who matched the rhythm of her sewing machine with the constancy of her complaints, voicing her many real and imaginary ailments.

This is not to say that Yvonne did not sew. She did indeed, as long as the condition of her pregnancies permitted. It was her lot also to cook, scrub, and do her housework, with occasional help from Tinonc or a neighbor and increasingly from the children as they grew older.

Among the Acadian women of this day, the hard-working lot of the housewife was an institution that no one even thought of abolishing. It was based in love, that sacrificial oblation which generated peace and happiness. Nor did anyone consider it necessary to lift the burden and sweat of the fields from the stooped shoulders of the men or from those of the young boys who tracked the dusty furrows with their sodden feet or squeezed the soft mud between their toes. Nor did complaints issue from the young girls who enfolded their bodies in long calico dresses, wrapped their heads and necks in flapping, sweaty old sunbonnets, and wore old discarded black stockings on their arms and ragged homemade mittens on their hands—all to mitigate the rigors of a merciless summer sun in the open shadeless fields.

22

Smith

Another of the local laboring class was the burly blacksmith. He was a friend of Tinonc's and spent fifteen hours of every day except Sunday in his shop in the small bend which the roadway made with the course of the bayou. His shop was ramshackle, one-walled, unpainted, but black with soot and ancient grime.

He and his shop were almost one in coloring, and the black smoke that he blew with his bellows respected neither him nor his walls. He worked his bellows and tongs with his left hand and with his right hand he poked the coals and wielded the big hammer that pounded the red metal on his ringing anvil.

When the metal cooled he poked it again deep into the red coals, extracting it as often as necessary until it was properly shaped or fused. He ended the process by tempering his steel (after a final reheating and hammering), dipping it cautiously and by degrees into a large wooden tub of cold water. The final touch was to place his material, if it needed an edge, into a vise and applying a heavy file up and down once or twice.

Little boys or girls delivered the material to the

smith and awaited in fascination the completion of his
work. If the work was *à crédit*, the *forgeron* made an
entry with heavy black fingers into a grimy account
book.

His name was Victor, and he talked incessantly in
a throated monotone without looking at his visitor or
customer. The little boys marvelled at his great
strength, while the little girls stood at a distance in
awe and fear. With his grip he could make any man
flinch—except Tinonc.

"*Bonjour*," says he to Tinonc. "We do not see
you often."

"Goo-od reason," says Tinonc. "You are so ugly
dat you hurt my eyes, an you work is so bad dat I do
my own at hoome. I am glad to see you laugh. I am
not joking. Wen you go hoome, *cher*, loo-ok in de
mirror and you will see Vic, de mos ugly face in de
whole world."

"Haw! haw! haw!" laughed Vic. "Listen to dat lil
man! Listen! *Ecoute*! Listen to dat man! Ugly? Who is
more ugly dan you, hein?"

"De trouble wit you, Vic, is dat you not only
ugly in de face but you head inside is empty."

"Say, Nonc," said Vic seriously, "how is de
family?"

"Goo-od," answered Nonc.

"You never be rich," said Vic, "you got too
many children. Now, Sosthène, him, had plenty, but
dey all die but one."

"I got a secret," said Nonc. "Also, de number of
my children is none of you business. Beat you plow-
point and swallow you smoke an sweat and stop
counting my children."

23

Problems

Again, the same old refrain, thought Tinonc, even from a friend of many years. Why could not people cease their incessant harping on a topic so distasteful and disturbing?

Of course it mattered to him whether or not he could properly rear his children, but why did it so concern others? How did they know his future so far in advance? Why the pessimism? Who knew his business? Could he not have invested a few hundred dollars in land or in oil and made mountains of money later? Did anybody know how much he saved and invested? Did anybody know anything about him for certain? Was farm tenancy eternal, with no hope of escape? Did not most people work for others?

It was a fact that thousands of acres of good but low and wooded lands in the civil parish could still be bought for five or ten dollars per acre. If he had made such an investment, would Victor, Sibec, Bouqueta, or anyone else know? What about mineral rights and oil or gas?

"Not by bread alone did man live," said his friend Tidoon, wishing to appear as learned as he was in fact irrelevant.

"He can eat potato," said Jean Ba, "hein Tidoon?"

"*Bien sûr*! Sure!" answered Victor.

"Loo-ok at Sibec down de road. Dat is a *pistolet*," offered Tidoon.

"He walk like a monkey," said Victor.

"If he not careful he will step on his hand," said Jean Ba.

"Perhap he could sell me some land for some frog an turtle; den I could also buy Jean Ba's land an make everybody stop talking. Den I could be rich an send my boys to de college wit potato an preserve an enough food to learn de lesson. To learn you mus eat."

He could easily joke but his problem remained.

"Who has no problem?" asked Yvonne when he reached home.

"You, *chère*, you. Only a house fool of little ones all a year apart; dey are no problem because you heart is so big an you are fool of courage. Even so, some day we will show dem. We will have a big surprise."

24

Yvonne Meets Tidoon

The economic depression moved across the thirties and finally ended with the war impetus, when the first of the Cajuns invaded the military campsites to labor as carpenters at wages they had never received before. The breath of change was blowing across the land. The new dollars would bring new businesses, new ideas, new people, new schools.

The young Acadian would begin to change, to learn more English, to learn more lessons, to move beyond the civil parish, to dream of other worlds away from the bayou. Many would try for a time to live in those worlds beyond, but would then leave and return with joy like prodigals to their homeland and their patrimony where the grass grew tall and thick and green.

Tinonc himself had never cared to travel. He had never set foot outside of his state. He had gone only once to New Orleans. Neither he nor Yvonne liked the slow trains that blew soot, cinders, and dust through the windows, that stopped at every station, that caked their foul breath in the creases of your neck.

They both remembered Jean Ba's daughter, Anne, when she bade her sad farewell to the village, on her way by train to nursing school in New Orleans.

They often talked about young Tidoon, now a man, whom Yvonne had disliked, for a time, for telling people that she had no teeth. He and Anne were married after her short stay in the city and the end of their lovers' quarrel.

One day when Yvonne was walking downtown on the board sidewalk with her penultimate son, she came upon young Tidoon. She had just tripped on a loose board and he had rushed, in chivalrous alarm, to offer assistance. At the moment of confrontation, she had fully regained her feet and stood looking into the eyes of this young man who was almost a stranger to her, since he had been away at school for so long. He was gracious, kind, and concerned, and she to him was unbelievable. What was hard for them both to believe was that both belonged to the village, each unknown to the other.

"Your husband has been my friend since I was a baby. As a child I remembered you at a distance, but I had no idea you were the person I've just discovered. I don't want to be fresh, but I must tell you: You are beautiful."

"Thank you for exaggerating. I do like compliments," she answered smiling. "Your Anne is very beautiful and much younger than I am. I'm an old woman with a house full of children."

"You look as young as Anne. How is Nonc?"

"As wonderful as ever," she boasted.

"One in a million," he said sincerely.

"I'll love you for saying it, and I'll surely tell him," she said, smiling.

At home Yvonne said to Tinonc, "What a fine man is Tidoon!"

"I love him like a brother," answered her husband.

"Do you know what he told me about you? You are one in a million."

"Dat is a big number," he answered.

She then told him more about her conversation with Tidoon. "How is Anne?" she had asked him.

"Wonderful," he had answered. "How can two, like you and Anne, live in one village?"

"I don't know. You could ask Tinonc; he is a mathematician."

"What I want you to know is that you are the most beautiful woman I have ever met. My Anne is runner-up. One other thing I must say—from all I know, you must be at least ten years older than Anne, but you look her age. At thirty, you're a young twenty."

"You are flattering an old woman with a house full of children—of her own."

Yvonne now asked her husband, "Do you really know Tidoon?"

"*Mais oui,* all my life."

When young Tidoon reached his father's home Papa Naquin said, "From where you come, *cher?*"

"From town, talking to a glamor girl."

"Wat girl?"

"Yvonne. I had seen her a thousand times but had never really looked at her."

"Is purty her, hein?"

"Pretty! She is beautiful," he exclaimed.

"But, my son, dat is not all. Loo-ok at her lil children. Loo-ok at Tinonc. For many year she teach Tinonc. She make him read many book, an de newspaper. All de children she put in one room every day

at a big table. She help each one wit school. De girls
have housework, de boys outside work. Dey study all
ensemble; not one can talk. You visit dem at night
from before supper until dey go to bed an you will
see—all happy."

"I will do that, my papa, and then tell Anne."

"De story of Yvonne is like a story book. Her
life is like a book, a goo-od one. I will tell you more
wen you come wit Anne. Now you have a wife; you
are interested. She, Yvonne, is not a boss. She is de
lover of everybody."

"Nobody could boss Tinonc, anyway," Tidoon
added.

"True," said Father Naquin.

25

Tidoon's and Tinonc's Families

And life moved on into the unknown future, into the great war that at first scarcely touched Acadiana except for the boys who went off to camp or crossed the oceans and came back wide-eyed to realize that everything in the bayou country was so much smaller and shorter and shallower than it had seemed before and so very, very quiet and slow. When would this unhurried land yield to the forces of modern progress? Who would make the change? Why? Would the nervous young ex-soldiers be the ones? Or would it be Naquin, father or son? How good was modern progress—unrestrained?

The attention of the village was increasingly focusing on young Naquin. Would he be the spur? Did he have the dynamism? Of course, no one knew the promises of the future. The course of history could be changed for better or for worse by the free will of man so prone to misjudge or misevaluate, especially a new technology or a new public moral concept.

Young Tidoon had the leadership ability and sufficient education to guide his people into the unknown. Did he have the will?

After visiting the family of Tinonc and Yvonne as directed by his papa, he had engaged a group in conversation.

"How come," asked Sibec, "how come Tinonc's children can be so goo-od?"

"How come?" echoed Madame.

"Very simple," answered Tidoon. "Look at the parents. Who's a nicer guy than Tinonc or a finer wife than Yvonne? We'd have no fears for the future of our people if all children were like theirs. You know those children, Sib; you know how they talk, how they work, how they laugh, how they study? Did you ever see little babies cook, clean house, wash dishes, take care of the littler ones? Did you ever see little boys work like men in the barnyard and around the house and in the field? Did you ever see them studying their lessons, saying their prayers, loving father, mother, and one another? It's unbelievable, but true. And still more wonderful is the fact that they all get straight As in school. Ain't that perfect?"

"You damn right!" said Sibec. "You damn right! Too bad he don got some money."

"Money for what?" asked Tidoon, fixing a hard look on Sibec.

"Money for wat?" asked Madame, not to be left out of the conversation.

"For to go to school," answered Sibec now shamefaced and crossing his eyes, conscious of having blundered.

"Let me tell you something," continued Tidoon. "These little girls are little women in a house. And the little boys, did you ever see them box, run, jump, play ball, chop wood, ride horses?"

"Not me, *non*, Tidoon," stammered Sibec, recovering.

"You know the genius of that family? Yvonne—with Tinonc, a fine team. Yvonne. She is smart, she is beautiful, she is good."

"What you got?" asked Arsène. "You ain't sweet on Yvonne, hein?"

Sibec quaked in his boots over the brazen impudence of that question and Madame edged behind her husband, peeping to assess Tidoon's reaction.

"Look here, you little pipsqueak, you worm!" With lightning on his face and thunder in his voice Tidoon threatened, "I'll let you live now, but if I ever know that you've talked like this again, I'll make you bite the dust and foam at the filthy mouth. Why can't you be decent, you stinking little monster? Get out of here! And be sure Tinonc doesn't know what you said. He'd crack every bone in your body."

Arsène turned and left. He would never learn. *Misère!*

"De only difference between him an a dog," Jean Ba had once said, "is dat he don got no tail."

"Nex time you want to talk, Jean Ba," his friend Tidoon, Sr. had added, "put up you han an get permission."

"Dat are not funny," Baba had rejoined.

"There's one other thing about Tinonc," continued the younger Tidoon. "Although a small man, he has a big brain. He understands and he never forgets. He went through the third grade, but he knows all of arithmetic. He can multiply big numbers without a pencil. Papa says he can go to the sales barn, buy a calf, and write a check before the sales ticket has been written. He's never wrong by more than five pounds or one dollar."

"Be damn?" said Sibec, scratching his head interrogatively. "He strong like hell, also, him," said Sibec.

"When I was a little boy, I asked my papa what Tinonc was made of, since his body was so hard. 'I tell you,' said my papa, 'when he eats supper, he puts cement with his cornbread and milk. That makes him hard as rock.' "

"Me, I do not battle wit Tinonc, me, Tidoon. *Non, non,* not me!" Jean Ba had offered.

26

From House to House

Nobody knew better than the Blanchards what Tinonc could do with numbers. M. Blanchard in his cumbersome advancing years was beginning to rely more and more on the abilities and skills of Tinonc, at least to confirm his business findings and general security. A very scrupulous and meticulous man was *Monsieur* Father-in-law—with his wife whining in the background. Very, very sick was *Madame*. Between cancer and being *poitrinaire*, she could not live more than a handful of years, even months, poor soul. She knew that for certain and she added tears in anticipation. That was why she prayed so much, *pauvre bête*.

Madame did get seriously ill and had to stay in bed for a whole month with a *pleurésie*. She got so weak in bed for so long that Sosthène had to pick her up in the morning after her recovery, just about every day except when he forgot, at which time she managed somehow to function properly in private without any assistance. It was *malheureux* beyond words.

When Madame finally died of pneumonia, it was a great surprise to everyone. Sosthène himself had not believed that she was so ill. Yet, he had often wondered how living bones could last so long—not being disrespectful.

Madame's one great delight had been Yvonne, whom she adored, the only one of eight offspring who had survived infancy. The *Bon Dieu* had given that girl everything that the other seven children might have lacked. Of course, Madame was not one to complain, since she could count her one blessing.

So much did she treasure Yvonne that she was ecstatic when she saw her again after a lapse of just one or two days. Her bony face would flush with pleasure. Sosthène himself was overjoyed to see his wife so thrilled.

Madame died in her sleep one night in her long, loose flannel nightgown, cuddled and cold against Sosthène's back.

He rushed to tell the nearest neighbor and then ran to Yvonne who brought two of her little girls to do the housework and two of the little boys to do *Pépère* Sosthène's yard work. Sosthène was sadly stricken, severed at last from his only close human attachment, one who had become a habit to him. What would he do without her?

All he could do in the house was to make coffee; in the kitchen by the hot wood stove, he was totally helpless and unhappy. There was nothing he disliked more than to sweat in the house. In the field, it was natural, and a wet shirt cooled you off. You did not smell too good, but you could not smell yourself anyway. He'd like to go live with Yvonne, but that house was full. Some of the children could come and live with him, but Yvonne and Tinonc would never permit them. Perhaps it was better to die: How could you die if you were not sick? God killed people when

He was good and ready. He didn't give reasons. You could go to the cemetery and buy a burial lot or just get a mason to build a tomb above your wife's, and then add your name to hers and the date later when God gave it.

"You papa is lost," said Tinonc to Yvonne.

"I know, *cher*," she answered, "but I don't know what to do. Perhaps two of the boys could go sleep with him after their lessons and work."

Life became a *misère* for Sosthène, and when grave illness struck him down he succumbed without a struggle. He had been working too hard and he was convinced that he had lived too long. The pneumonia that took him was still a killer in his day. All his affairs were in perfect order, ready for transfer to Yvonne and Tinonc.

It is interesting to note that not even Sosthène had known about the "cypress house" where Tinonc had worked for so many years. The purchase of that house and 500 acres of land had come as a complete surprise to the villagers.

"*Pensez donc!*" said Sibec, "Jus five dollar an acre," when the full story finally came out.

No one could have guessed that Tinonc's interest across the years had been anything but a phase of service to du Clozal. He was so often seen repairing fences, airing the big house, at times accompanied by Yvonne and the children. People believed that he was only repaying du Clozal for countless benefactions.

What they did not know was that du Clozal owed much more than he could ever repay to Tinonc.

It was on a bright day in early November, when the first north winds had cooled the warm bayou water, that du Clozal, while casting for bass, had overturned his little dugout in midstream. Although a vigorous swimmer, he had taken only a few strokes when cramps immobilized him and brought him underwater.

Tinonc, on the bank, saw him go under and fail to surface more than once. Only a man of the swamps and the bayous could correctly assess a situation made doubly bad by a swift current. Tinonc ran downstream for some fifty paces, then dove in, heading towards a partly submerged tree, where he judged his friend might be lodged.

As luck and experience would have it, he had taken a bee-line for the man's body. Quickly Tinonc pulled it up and released it from the debris where it was fastened. The head he raised above water, swimming backwards to reach the shore. Then he turned the long body over and fixed it at mid-section upon his knee. He checked the mouth and found it in proper condition to resume breathing.

How cheap was life! How vulnerable was man! "My friend," he soliloquized, shedding tears, "you don't know how far gone you are, how much at God's mercy."

Some of the water gushed out of the body's mouth. Hopefully Tinonc resumed the mechanics of pressure and release and saw his friend twitch his eyelids in responsive life.

After a few minutes and when he was certain that he was safe, he took his friend and brought him home to Yvonne who summoned the old doctor.

"So, it's your will," said the doctor, "that nobody should know about this accident. I've kept many professional secrets before, and I'll keep this one, but, boy, I can tell you, if I had done what you did, Nonc,

I'd go blow my horn all over town." To Yvonne he said, "Let him stay here a day or two and I'll tell his sick wife that he and Nonc went hunting—since you need the secret. *Au revoir*, my friends."

Thus du Clozal had incurred the greatest debt possible to man and ever afterwards did all that he could to repay his friend. There had always been affection between the two, but henceforth the older man viewed his friend with a sort of reverence.

When his daughter, Marie Anne, saw her father, she fell upon the bed, embraced him and shed tears of joy. With shining eyes she embraced Tinonc.

When *Madame* du Clozal came to her husband, he was so well he could himself give her a full account of the rescue. "Only Tinonc could have saved him," she said. "It was God's providence."

It was a sort of shyness that compelled Tinonc to request silence with regard to the rescue of his friend. The role of hero was very distasteful to him, because it so often entailed embarrassing answers to unnecessary questions. Besides, he saw no heroism in diving to save a friend when he had so often done as much to earn fifty cents or less. True, a man's life was priceless, but was it not a fact that it was risked every minute of every day and night? Was not man so vulnerable and so much exposed to so many hazards that it was a wonder he survived for as long as he did?

27

Time Marches On

The years that followed the war were years of change, of vast scientific, technological, economic, and social developments across the land. The little cabins that hugged the woodside or squatted amid the corn and cottonfields, began to release their tenants, who packed their household effects, with soiled mattresses and chicken coops, and moved by pickup or wagon into the villages, towns, and cities.

The mules and horses that walked the single furrows were gradually nudged out by tractors that grew in size until their final evolution into the high, wide mechanical monsters that could replace dozens of men and mules—and the little cabins became mere storage places for hay or implements. It was all a vast, uncontrolled exodus that headed in all directions in search of a better life and even of survival.

Some men went offshore, leaving their wives and children in the villages and towns. They brought more dollars from the oil fields but saw the passing of their culture, which was priceless.

Meanwhile the roads and lanes had become highways, asphalted, concreted, two-laned, four-laned. The cattle that grazed on the shoulders were driven home to fences and feed lots.

The buggies began vanishing and the loud, high-stepping little cars gave way to bigger and sleeker and costlier conveyances. The little trucks were replaced by giants with huge trailer appendages, their drivers sitting in the clouds. The little first-grader had as many as eighteen big tires to count as the big diesels roared by.

Farmers were using crossties from abandoned railroads to build tight fences to contain their elegant cows.

Then the race tracks came, filling the countryside with shiny thoroughbreds and quarterhorses and roadside lounges.

Was it a fair trade to give the peace and simplicity of the past for multiple, nameless, and pervasive pollution?

28

Homework

Often at nightfall in their bedroom, Tinonc and Yvonne sat together listening to the soft exchanges of the children at their studies. This was a routine, first in the cramped little hallway of their tenant cabin, next in the Blanchard kitchen, and finally in the dining room of the big house.

While in the tenant cabin the children were quite small. Their study table was long and of coarse boards and lighted by two kerosene lamps. The two benches on which they sat had no backs. In the cabin they were all quite small and more or less one year, one grade apart, and there were always at least two pre-schoolers who at the daily beginning of home study were most often fast asleep in their cradles.

There were often squabbles demanding resolution either by the eldest girl, named Yvonne and called Y, or by the youngest boy of school age, named Jean and called Ti (for Tinonc) because of his close resemblance to his father. Ti was a very industrious first-grader, a leader of men, who toppled his classmates and many upperclassmen on the playground just as his father had done before him.

In the family he bossed all the children above

and below him, all except Y. Sometimes he used a hand so heavy as to require the intervention of Tinonc or Yvonne. The bawling of a brother or sister might grow loud enogh to rupture the peace of the whole household.

"Ti!" cried Papa Tinonc, "Wat de trouble?"

"What did you do wrong?" asked Yvonne.

"He took my pencil an he hit me," said the weeping elder brother.

"Did you?" asked Mama Yvonne.

"Yes, Mama, but he was make faces at me."

"Making, *cher*, not make."

"He making faces at me," he answered.

"He *was* making," corrected the mother again.

"He was making," Ti responded.

"Did those faces hurt you?" she asked.

"No, Mama."

"Then, who is bad?" she asked.

"Me, Mama."

"Come," said Papa Tinonc. "Come, Ti! Get my switch, *cher*. Papa will whip you. Why?"

"Because I am bad," he answered.

"An you brother, must I whip him also?"

"No, Papa."

"Yes, Papa," answered the brother. "Give me two licks."

"Touch you toes," said Papa.

"One, two; now Ti, ten for you—one, two, three, four five—*assez*—five? *Oui*." Come, *bébé*, let Papa kiss you. You know, without love I cannot whip you." The little boy, sobbing, fell into his father's arms, then hugged and kissed his mother and his brother victim, and returned to the study table smiling while both parents shed a tear.

In the Blanchard house, the routine was more or less the same except for natural variations in growth, maturity, and numbers.

Ti especially had to be cautioned and taught not to fight at the drop of anybody's hat and not to take advantage of another's weakness.

One day Papa Tinonc overheard a muffled conversation and unusual giggling among the children.

"Tell Papa, *cher!*" he called to Ti who was now in the third grade.

"What did you do?" asked Mama Yvonne, who always worked as a disciplinary team with her husband.

"It is a man on his way to school who make his boy fight. A new man, Papa."

"What did you do?" repeated Mama.

"I do not want to fight, but his papa push him," he answered.

"And what did you do?" Mama continued asking.

"Well, wen he swing I catch his arms and squeeze dem an he cry because it hurt. His mad papa pull his ear, an say, '*Allons!*' I am sorry, Papa," he concluded.

"Why?" asked Tinonc chuckling.

"Because he cannot fight."

When the family moved into their third home, the house was much bigger and more than enough to contain the diminishing ever-changing group of brothers and sisters.

29

The Big House
and the People

In the family no one had changed less than
Yvonne. Her body remained slim and trim and her
features were still unblemished, almost untouched by
the merciless fingers of time. She still retained the
beauty that Tidoon had discovered many years before
on that chance meeting on the board sidewalk.

After moving into the Blanchard home which he
had inherited, after the doubling of the family income,
after the death of du Clozal and his wife—the family
was ready at last to move into the big house on the
bayou, some four miles from town.

It was a cool day in the beginning of fall when
Yvonne and Tinonc revisited their new home before
their final moving day. God's wind was playing all
around the house and sweeping under it and whistling
at a lazy gray cat sitting on a broken brick pillar
beneath, cocking its green-eyed head to figure what
these unwanted people could be looking for—surely
not for rats, because they were all still in the fields,
fat and contented and tasty.

The two still looked young.

In front of the old house were two huge liveoak trees spreading their long horizontal limbs across nearly two acres of lawn. The oak limbs almost met above a brick walk aimed at the wide steps of the porch which extended the whole length of the house.

The couple paused to observe the cat who was casting a wary, predatory eye on a screech owl perched on a limb in the obscurity of one of the great oaks. Often the cat and the owl competed for the mice that came for winter and coziness after the crop fields were cold and bare.

Yvonne held Tinonc's hand and they walked closely as lovers do. Once on the porch he kissed her on the lips. Then he opened the front door and both stepped inside. The house was in order except for dust that had resettled on pieces of broken antique chairs and on old French newspapers in the living room. Yvonne's probing fingers were dusty, too.

"Some on your nose," said Tinonc. He kissed it and got his tongue muddy.

This house belonged to another century. The baseboards and floorboards were wide, the ceilings high; the door and window frames were ornamented, the walls plastered. There were fireplaces in all the rooms, a hand water-pump in the kitchen. This was the "cypress house," made of ancient tide-water cypress. There was no paint on the exterior except on the porches and under the eaves. It was a story and a half, with two wide dormers sitting atop the front roof like eyes looking towards the highway and the concurrent bayou.

Once again under the great oaks some two weeks later the same couple stood, looking at a full assembly of the people of St. Pierre—men, women, and children, generations, two, three, four, and five indiscriminately mixed and milling around, as people always do on such occasions. This was the annual fun and fund-raising event for the benefit of the single village civic club and the church. All the families brought food and then bought it back at two dollars per adult person and one dollar per child. The merriment and the camaraderie were free.

Among the crowd were the very old, with tired, nearsighted eyes and uncertain feet. Playing by them were the babies, who toddled and slobbered and drooled wet, muddy streaks across their white shirts and blackened their damp seats by sitting in the dust, *pensez donc!*

There was a bearded little old man who cocked his head when he talked, who joked about everybody, grinning a shy, labored little grin that made everybody laugh—Jean Ba.

Here, too, was a corpulent woman who had come out of New Orleans many years before, a big blonde, once buxom, now grown hefty—with two young sons in tow. She talked in a loud voice, without a touch of Cajun accent. She would say, "What the hell!" and still try to look "cute." With her, this Irma Cook, was her small native husband who relished vulgarities and liked his wife's female cousin who was younger, flashy, and sexy. This family group, though part of the assemblage, did not seem to fit, any of them, especially the young boys, who threw rocks and twigs in all directions with gusto and impunity—until Tinonc collared them with a warning and a shoulder grip that made them wince and whimper and desist.

Another man of late middle age, dignified, hanc

some and bold, walked with a younger man who could have been a twin except for age. These two looked and talked and walked like men of authority and success—the Tidoon Naquins, *père* and *fils*. Along with and surrounding the pair was a bevy of young girls such as might be seen at a mixed high school and elementary school recess. By their looks these were all of one family—daughters, grandchildren, first cousins. On the perimeter of the distaff group was a group of boys, apparently equal in number and likewise of evident consanguinity. All were Naquins and Noëls paternally and maternally.

Beyond and to the rear were the young Lanclos, running from their vehicles to merge with their cousins and friends.

Up nearer the house was Tinonc's family, older now, two of them married and all of them on special behavior for the occasion.

A distinctively unhandsome pair were Eusèbe and Grand Rouge, Eusèbe having lost his wife and his last tooth and chewing his gums incessantly. His shoulders were more stooped than ever and his long back showed a median line of little bumps under his shirt. His ready laugh made his body shake and quiver. His companion's eyes were green in a setting of splotched red. He chewed tobacco and maintained a short streak of dried juice in the wrinkled corners of his mouth.

The Sibecs were together as always, the man leading the way as always, and the woman following in instinctive submission, like a tired old rabbit hound, *pauvre bête*. They both looked all around as if in partisan search of topics for storage and reserve for future fault-finding.

Victor, the blacksmith, followed upon the heels

of Madame Sibec. Papa Naquin said that Vic looked like somebody else outside of his shop. He was as clean as the soap and cold water in a washtub in his kitchen could make him, all except for the black compounds that ordinary scrubbing could not remove from battered fingernails.

All of the assembled people spoke French, some of them not a word of English; most of them, young and middle-aged and old, mixed French and English in a unique way, beginning a sentence with one language and ending it with another. The present mobility and affluence of the people had made it possible for every villager to attend this annual picnic, even at a distance of four miles. In earlier days, all public functions were within walking distance of the residences. It had been the custom to rotate the location of the festival from one suitable place to another. By exception on this occasion, it came to Tinonc out of rote and out of town, by reason of the exceptional atmosphere and of other considerations advanced and determined by Tidoon, Jr.

Speakers

The man ascending the platform was Tidoon
Naquin, Jr., the happy firebrand of the upper Teche
country, the same who had but recently refused to
run for governor to the disappointment of many
friends throughout Acadiana. The people applauded as
he signalled for their attention, and continued their
applause when Tinonc joined him on the platform.

"Be damn!" said Sibec, "not Tinonc gonna make
a speech?"

"*Messieurs, mesdames, et mes chers amis,*" said
Tidoon in imitation of *Cousin* Dudley LeBlanc, the
late Hadacol supersalesman, "and all you bright young
and old *cousins* and *cousines*. I am so happy to be
here to tell you all I know about St. Pierre since this
time a year ago. This has been our custom. For this
reason I'll talk first about Tinonc, our friend and the
faithful friend of *Msieu* du Clozal, the man who sold
him ·his beautiful estate which, as you know, once
beloᵣ ǵed to a du Clozal cousin and which without
Γinoɴ.'s help was considered a surplus burden and a
liabiliₜ,. Γinonc, for many years, refused to give away
the gₗ ₐt secret of his relationship to *Msieu* du Clozal,
ᴏut ɴ. ₐᵥ. after a five-day battle on my part, he has

reluctantly consented to let me tell you that he once saved his good friend's life. Pierre and Marie Anne will bear me out in telling you how he rescued *Msieu* from drowning in the bayou in front of this very house, how he and Yvonne kept him in their home until discharged by the doctor. You all know what I think of Tinonc, of his wife, of all his children. Give him a big hand, *mes amis*. Give it to Yvonne, the lovely lady who has borne his children and walked beside him, as trim and as fair today as she was twenty years ago.

"You, my papa, clap for Tinonc, and you, Baba. You Eusèbe, you Pierre, you Marie Anne, you Victor, you everybody from St. Pierre. It is only because of modesty and honesty that he has refused to accept public acclaim for heroism. I made him see that his valor belongs to his family. Nonc has had a hard life, as you know, and he deserves every bit of his success.

"It has always been our custom to have a speaker for this occasion. I am a poor substitute, not a real speaker but one making Cajun noises with my mouth and lungs. For what I am worth, I hope you will hear me and hear all the others who will follow me.

"Many of us remember Nonc as a young barefoot boy before he knew one word of English. We saw him often come out of the *cyprière* with a wet muddy sack on his back—a little boy who braved a big man's dangers.

"We remember when he grew up and married Yvonne—the young man who was already raising a family and who was ready to start another. Today he sits here upon this platform and squirms as I praise him. He looks down and sees his children standing near their mother and wondering what this Tidoon has in store for their papa.

"Now, I'll ask Nonc to give you a few words of greeting. Later, he'll have much more to say. Tinonc, my friend, speak."

"Tidoon is smart," said Nonc, "and he talks well, but sometimes his talking is like a big bird. It has wings and flies through the clouds. He was flying high just now. The Tinonc I know is just a plain little man, not the man of Tidoon's words. I had a hard life, it is true, but *merci Bon Dieu*, ever since Yvonne it is beautiful. I was weak and hopeless; she made me want to be strong. I became an alcoholic, but now for years, I drink *water*. I thank God for my children; they are hers, too. I am proud of them, but the great pride of my life is my wife. I am looking at her. There are tears in her eyes. I am proud of her tears. God bless you, people of St. Pierre. I am proud of you, too."

Tinonc received such thunderous applause that he decided he was through and sat down.

"Now," said Tidoon, "we'll ask my papa to come up."

"Imagine," said papa, "an ole man like me make a speech. My French is bad, my Cajun is worser, an my English is not *civilizé*. If I speak French, my bes friend, Baba, will not unerstand; if I speak Cajun the children will laugh, and if I continue in English, everybody will leave to start eating before it is time. Wat mus I do?"

"Sing, Tidoon, sing. Sing 'Bonsoir Rosalie.' "

"Sing 'La fille à Philogène.' "

"No, my friends, I cannot sing. My voice is cracked an weak. Instead of a song, I will call Jean Ba. Come up, Baba."

Jean Ba was so prodded by his neighbors that he could not escape.

"Now, my friends," continued Tidoon. "Come here Baba. *Comme ça.* Let me show them how pretty you long white beard is. Speech, Baba."

"Speech Baba."

"Tidoon," said Baba, "is all de time to make a farce on my beard, him. Look, people, he got wrinkles on his face but I have none."

Jean Ba rushed off the platform laughing out loud—for once.

Next was Pierre Lanclos, whom all the school children called Professor. He indicated that the occasion was for others, not for him; that Tinonc was a prime example of how much a person could learn out of school. Of course, not every man was lucky enough to have an Yvonne to help. "And since you already know one of Tinonc's secrets, I'll tell you another. He once saved my life, too, from drowning, when we were little boys. And yet another secret. You know the little talk he gave a while ago; he recited it to me for help, if needed. There was not a single word wrong. My advice to all the young school people here today is to learn as Tinonc did. Of course, don't quit school in the third grade. You are not Tinoncs any of you. There's only one.

"Tidoon, *cher*, you take over again."

"Yvonne," called young Tidoon as Pierre stepped down. "Come up, Yvonne, you and all your children and your two sons-in-law."

Yvonne stepped up after counting her nine plus two. She kissed Tinonc as the people roared approval. She turned towards them and said, "God bless you!" and continued, "I am sure you'd like to hear our two friends sing. May I ask them in your name to sing at least two or three of our Cajun songs? Our good friend Jean Ba and my husband, too, will sing with them."

"Off key!" said young Tidoon.

"Sing! Sing! *Chantez!*" shouted the people with one voice.

Under such compulsion the men had no choice and the powerful voices of the two Naquins flowed through the assembly.

It was but the following day, ill-fated foggy morning, that Tinonc went hunting and a deer hunter put a bullet through his heart, and all the people, happy and laughing one day, were weeping the next.

Thus ended the life of Tinonc the invulnerable, Tinonc, the little man who had braved a thousand dangers almost from birth. *Incroyable!* Such a little bullet! Such a long chance!

Who in St. Pierre could believe that Tinonc was dead? *Quel malheur!* Poor Yvonne! Good, anyway, that he was not a witness of his own death. He who had seen so many others in death. He who was so well acquainted with tragedy—in his own close family!

It was odd that Ti, the son who resembled him the most, would be the one to stand beside his stricken mother in the full power of precocious manhood as Tinonc himself had done for his widowed mother and fatherless family many years before.

After the funeral, Jean Ba said to Tidoon, Sr., "I have a thought, Tidoon."

"Does it hurt?" asked young Tidoon.

"You Tidoon, you will make you papa make a farce on my beard." Turning to the senior Naquin, he said, "You know wat, Tidoon? I bet Tinonc can sing better dan you, now, him."

"So true!" answered Tidoon very solemnly.

FIN

Appendix

J'ai Passé Devant Ta Porte

The lyric, or text, of this all-time favorite Cajun song spells out a very tragic event—that of a young boy who suddenly and quite unexpectedly finds out that his bride-to-be has died. Throughout the years since its origin (date unknown), the element of sadness still remains, thus giving the Cajun a vent for expression of a very deep-seated emotion, basic to all humanity. The emotional impact, however, is not particularly restricted to the original text, but can (and usually does) reflect a tinge of sadness. Invariably, when Cajuns gather to sing, dance, and have a good time, this song will be among the first to be sung.

1. *J'ai passé devant ta porte.*
   J'ai crié, "Bye, bye," la belle.
   'Ya personne qui m'a répondu.
   Oo yé, 'yaie, mon coeur fait mal.

2. *J'm'ai donc mis à observer.*
   Moi, j'ai vu une 'tite lumière allumée.
   Il ya que'que chose qui m'disait j'aurais pleuré.
   Oo yé, 'yaie, mon coeur fait mal.

3. *Moi, j'ai été cogner à la porte.*
   Quand ils m'ont ouvert la porte,
   J'ai vu des chandelles allumées,
   Tout le tour de son cercueil.

4. (Repeat first verse.)

Allons Danser, Colinda**

The Cajuns, in spite of their hard work, troubles and tragedies, always seemed to find time to enjoy themselves, especially on Saturday nights. After such a night of revelry, most, if not all, were very faithful in their church attendance on Sunday. This song, a real "foot-stomper," was (and still is) one of their favorite dancing tunes.

Although the words may upon first reading seem somewhat suggestive, such is not the case. In fact, in keeping with the stiff traditions of the times, it reflects the younger people's attempts to outwit the older generation.

1. *Allons danser, Colinda,*
Allons danser, Colinda,
Allons danser, Colinda,
Pour faire fâcher les vieilles femmes,
Allons dan-tan-dis ta mère nous voit pas.

2. *Allons danser, Colinda,*
Danser collés, Colinda,
Allons danser, Colinda,
Pour faire fâcher les vieilles femmes.
C'est pas tout l'monde qui connaît
Danser les danses du vieux temps,
Allons danser, Colinda,
Pour faire fâcher les vieilles femmes.

The vocal is invariably interspersed with instrumental solos on the violin and/or accordion, until the musicians finally decide to stop.

**Some controversy exists as to the original and true intent of this song. There are some who say that it is a young boy asking his girl friend to dance with him, while others contend that the song itself refers to a specific kind of dance (the Calinda). This author prefers the first interpretation.

116

Mon Bon Vieux Mari

This song is a "tongue-in-cheek" dialogue between wife and husband and is really nonsensical in intent. It is typical of the Cajun's humor, especially the ability to laugh at himself.

The wife sings the verses, and the husband answers (rather gruffly) in between.

1. *Et où c'est que t'es parti, mais, mon bon vieux mari?*
   Et où c'est que t'es parti ça qu'on appelle l'amour?
   Et où c'est que t'es parti, mais, mon bon vieux mari?
   Le meilleur buveur du pays!
       Parti au cafe!*

The remaining verses are virtually the same except for the one line which changes (including slight variations in the melodic pattern to accommodate the words). The other verses are:

2. *Qu'est-ce que t'es*
   parti faire, mais, mon bon vieux mari?
   Parti me souler!*

3. *Et quand tu t'en reviens, mais, mon bon vieux mari?*
   Demain ou un autre jour!

4. *Mais, quoi tu veux j'te cuise, mais, mon bon vieux mari?*
   Trois douzaine d'oeufs et trois gallons d'couche-couche!

5. *Ça pourrait bien te tuer, mais, mon bon vieux mari.*
   Ça ne fait pas rien! C'est ça j'veux, mourir quandmême!

---

*Here, "Je suis" at the beginning of the responses is implied, but not actually spoken.

6. *Et où tu veux je t'enterre, mais, mon bon vieux mari?*
Dans le coin du foyer, et à tout moment passe-moi une patate chaude!

SONG TRANSLATIONS**

J'ai Passé Devant Ta Porte
(I Passed in Front of Your Door)

1. I passed in front of your door.
   I cried out, "Goodbye," my love.
   No one answered me.
   "Oo, yé, yaie," my heart aches.*

2. I then set myself to observe.
   I saw a little light (candle) lighted.
   Something told me I should be crying.
   "Oo, yé, yaie," my heart aches.

3. I went and knocked on the door.
   When they opened the door for me,
   I saw the candles lighted,
   All around your coffin.

4. (Same as first verse.)

Allons Danser, Colinda
(Let's Go Dance, Colinda)

1. Let's go dance, Colinda,
   Let's go dance, Colinda,
   Let's go dance, Colinda,
   To make the old ladies mad.
   Let's go dance, Colinda,
   While your mother doesn't see us.

2. Let's go dance, Colinda,
   Dance close together, Colinda,
   Let's go dance, Colinda,
   To make the old ladies mad.
   It's not everyone who knows how
   To dance the old time dances,

*The expression "Oo, yé, yaie," is simply that: an
expression, generally indicating pain.
**These translations are very loose, and not intended to be literal. Only
the essential meaning is given.

Let's go dance, Colinda,
To make the old ladies mad.

Mon Bon Vieux Mari
(My Good Old Husband)

1. Where are you going, my good old husband?
   Where are you going, my own true love?
   Where are you going, my good old husband?
   The best drinker in the land!
   (I am) Going to the saloon!

2. What are you going to do, my good old husband?
   (I am) Going to get drunk!

3. And when are you coming back?
   Tomorrow or another day!

4. Well, what do you want me to cook for you?
   Three dozen eggs and three gallons of couche-couche!

5. That could very well kill you.
   That doesn't matter! That's what I want, to die anyway!

6. Where do you want me to bury you?
   In the corner of the fireplace, and every now and then pass me a hot sweet potato!

Glossary

A credit—*on credit*
Affaire—*business*
A la maison—*at home*
Allons—*let's go*
Assez—*enough*
Bal de noces—*wedding dance*
Ballottement—*rocking, shaking*
Basse-cour—*poultry yard*
Bébé—*baby*
Bien sûr—*surely*
Bonjour—*good day*
Boudin—*Cajun sausage of blood (rouge), of highly seasoned rice (blanc)*
Bouteille—*bottle*
Boutique—*shop*
Charogne—*carrion*
Chantez—*sing*
Cher—*dear*
Chère pitié—*would you believe*
Chérie—*dearie*
Coin—*corner*
Comme ça—*thus*
Coup d'pied—*kick*
Cyprière—*cypress swamp*

Des petites toutoutes en rubans—*little beribboned girlies*

Défunte—*late*
Dépense—*pantry*
Do-do—*sleep*
Ecoute—*listen*
En amour—*in love*
Encore—*again*
Enfin—*finally*
Fais-do-do—*Cajun dance*
Faux pas—*mistake*
Fils—*son, junior*
Forgeron—*blacksmith*
Formidable—*unbelievable*
Garçon—*boy*
Garçonnière—*attic bedroom for boys*
Gar'soleil—*Acadian sunbonnet*
Gomme de mer—*black chewing gum*
Incroyable—*unbelievable*
Merci Bon Dieu—*thank God*
Père—*father, senior*
Pauvre bête—*poor fellow*
Régulateur—*regulator (liver)*
Remèdes simples—*simple remedies*
Savon d'pays—*homemade soap*
Tout d'suite—*right away*
Vilain—*ugly*
Voilà—*there, or there is*